Other Books in The Vintage Library
of Contemporary World Literature

PERSEPHONE

PERSEPHONE
Homero Aridjis

Translated from the revised Spanish edition
by Betty Ferber

AVENTURA

The Vintage Library of Contemporary World Literature

VINTAGE BOOKS · A DIVISION OF RANDOM HOUSE · NEW YORK

AN AVENTURA ORIGINAL, January 1986
Translation copyright © 1986 by Betty Ferber

All rights reserved under International and Pan-American Copyright
Conventions. Published in the United States by Random House, Inc., New
York, and simultaneously in Canada by Random House of Canada
Limited, Toronto. Originally published in Spanish as *Perséfone* by Editorial
Joaquín Mortiz, S.A., Tabasco (Mexico), in 1967; revised edition published
in 1986. Copyright © 1967, 1986 by Editorial Joaquín Moritz, S.A.
FIRST AMERICAN EDITION

Library of Congress Cataloging in Publication Data

Aridjis, Homero.
  Persephone.

  (Aventura)
  Translation of: Perséfone.
  1. Persephone (Greek deity)—Fiction. I. Title.
PQ7297.A8365P413   1986   863   85-40321
ISBN 0-394-74175-7

Book design by Joe Marc Freedman

Manufactured in the United States of America

PERSEPHONE

The night opens out: a flurry of legs.
    Colors, sounds open out.
The moment opens.
The vision is opening out.
Image by image.
The gaze is there: corroborating and forgetting, reborn and echoing.
The vision is opening out.
It acquires words, bodies that take root and footsteps that never will.
It advances bit by bit, simmering.

Night, young novice, old whore tracking passersby, will pause as usual at the brothel to nest, to deposit larva.
The music opens out, pleasure, squalor.
Capsules of insomnia, terror, malevolence.
Beings open up in a gesture, a sentence, a yawn.

The minute burns.
Burns up useful and useless alike.
Burns laughter, what isn't done, all movement.

Lips open like petals.
They utter opaque, multicolored words.
They flower and the petals drop.

• • •

Night grows over the city in women's small voices.
In women's scarlet breath.
In women's pendulous displayed fruits. Through women's
graves it tunnels into darkness. Through openings, voids and
holes, night penetrates and moistens.

The clock's hands buzz.
Thought, sadness, anger buzz.
Nostalgia for what hasn't been, light beating its wings in
memory's lair.

They talk sitting around tables, walking backwards, dancing
in circles, coupling without pity.
The pictures, the walls are talking.
Even the roots groping underground are talking.
Only what's missing is silent, what we dreamed would last.

Night walks the streets. It sports a wintry face and pale
legs.
It stalks through refuges, through theatres, with sure-footed
determination and assured expression.
Corseted and gauzy, night beckons from street corners, from
half-opened doors, from I'm-not-the-one-who's-calling, with a
certain lassitude.
Or like a desolate blotch, female and singular, rattles its
loose change, its high heels, its laughter.
Dressed up in many colors night heads for the brothel.
Flaunts scratched cheeks, unsatisfied pursuit, a fugitive
March and April in the offing.

• • •

A concavity, it collects hands, faces, postures.
It sleeps on its back in hotels, in fetal position in the
bedroom.
It hides in the closet if a fire is lit or when love approaches.
In a child's dream it weaves spiders and useless toys; it
weaves real elves and maternal abysses.
It coughs out broken hours in the room across the hall, or
falls apart and comes together again in a corner of the
brothel, or ghostlike can't pass through light.

It covers and uncovers mouths, feelings and chairs, belts and
smoke, nursing breasts and breasts as showy as moons.
Arms, knees and chins, squinty oblique eyes, tables,
shoes and hellos, glasses, cigarettes and caresses nest in its
belly.
Pants, vests, thighs and shoelaces, trays and words, slivers of
broken nails, gusts of euphoria and gusts of tenderness.

Persephone in profile has an odd way of looking sideways,
virginal and combative.
When she opens her wallet a chromo of a pointy-chinned
Son of God slips out. The explanatory caption says he
absolves joy through suffering.
A bum gave it to her as a dubious talisman.
To keep her from sinning with her face or with her tongue.

Smoke rises from her head, a vain saint's head, from her
flesh splintered by clumsy woodcutters, out of the hereditary
mole staring darkly on her neck.
Smoke emerges continuous and turbulent from her mouth,
like and unlike as a double-faced deity.

The smoke of her intimacy is consumed within, seeps
through her pores, brazenly prowls naked around the
brothel.
She can't find space enough for her body, nor body for all
the space she could fill.

She sways her shoulders and turns her head.
Sitting on a man's lap: glass in one hand like a chalice, belt
in the other hand like a cane.
She seems to understand people's rhythms, organs' vitality,
their erosion, their decline.
Dressed in red with bare legs, rings, necklaces and an
absence of shoes.
She ignores the murmuring laughing customers and the
cavorting tune that shatters something secret in the air. And
the sweating floozie to her right who yawns.
She only notices apathy crushing her in its masculine arms.

The music scatters, bounces off the walls, off buttocks and
feet of heavy and nimble whores.
It crackles, urges, provokes. Loses itself in meanders of
euphoric melancholy.
Softly returns.
Half-asleep nearly neuter customers roused by its influx look
about as if grasping at the sound, chasing but not catching it.
Weary faces exhibit creeping anxiety, flaccid staginess; lust
drools from their lips.
Brassy moments fall from the ceiling. A timetable of
penumbra and noise descends, a song of embraces.
This entoned time floats on the smoke, auguring rain, a mild
season, a ship sailing towards a dawn framed by waves, an
island at its center.

. . .

Laughter and yawns ring out during the breaks. Pleasures,
grievances, chagrin come and go.
A fire engine's siren complains resonantly, like burning
tinder.
I step forward. I retreat. I touch the table, my eyes, an
ashtray full of butts.
Men and women talking about some people I know
approach. They stop when they think I can hear them. They
back off and go on talking. Flushed, they fan their faces.
Mrs. Pavese lifts her skirt, tucks a bill between thigh and
garter, tightens an earring.
I feel Susi's moist coldness blowing on the nape of my neck.
I stare at the others. I dissemble. I look her straight in the
face. She moves away pretending not to see me.
I look for Susana, or a body to fill her name. Neither Marta
nor Maria have her eyes. She doesn't exist, so a whore
couldn't inhabit her. I look for bowlegged Carlota. I find
traces, a breast pressed against my arm like a piece of
rubber sticking to my flesh, aware of itself through me. I
turn to see who it is. But the girl, sensing my glance,
withdraws.

Familiar features surface in the penumbra. Outlines of faces
and hands. Jewelry. Puny men stamping to the rhythm, as if
dreamt by someone asleep inside them. Women aging
quickly watch far from themselves, from a century ago or
from the next century, from a life that passed by without
stopping or hasn't arrived yet.
Colors, sounds, pants and chairs change places. A musical
giddiness rises to the ceiling, a smoldering passage of time.
A few bulbs hang near the columns, shedding reddish light

in a meager circle. Here and there chins, shut eyelids, brown hands wearing golden, silvery or copper rings appear. Thighs loosely covered by thin materials are glimpsed. Three naked necks, white and rounded, seem to be offering themselves to the knife's cutting edge. A bare foot stands out of the shadows.

A musician sings of someone else's sorrow, a painless lament.

A red lantern sways in the background, lighting up the pine bar, a few plastic glasses, the noses and cheekbones of a group of whores seated there drinking.

Leaning against a column the brothel's owner gives orders to waiters, signals to a flabby whore exactly what she may and may not do. He nods yes or no, virtually hidden from the customers and from all who don't expect any sign from him. He is all eyes, all ears, his blood steady in his cheeks, his eyes steady in their orbits and his hair slicked back.

But I can count his faces and his masks; I pluck off his thoughts, his good fortune, his boredom. In him I see the bridge builder, the insurance salesman, the poker player: sitting by the window, sniffing at the behinds and ears of young girls who laugh from time to time, consenting.

In his hands I see the hands of a masseur unhooking a middle-aged woman's bra, his member growing hard blindly below, as he murmurs two or three words about the bad weather.

I see him there, like a sleeper trying to escape into a dream, who once inside it finds only himself again.

The musicians play a tango. Surrounded by the other six, the weakest one, like a standard clock, beats out the whine.

Beats uniform freedom, the anonymity of one hundred faces, a community of calves, chests and shoulders. Keeps time for a dancing cluster where the shortest disappear and the tallest stand out like grinning pickets.
Notes of fire and snow burn and dissolve, moan red-hot in the air or blanched turn to water in a corner.
Music is in the glasses and on the walls. A red sound drops from the ceiling, a song spotted with gray smoke rings, a blue density that exits whispering.
Shadows are audible. Colors move noisily. The night is a loud, populous phantom.

I hear a passing voice, the color yellow, the color green, the livid hour. A curving hip, a hollow laugh.
I see gestation and growth of the spider's strands, how the pubescent girl's belly fills with healthy noonday, how the dry goods jobber loses his teeth, and his memory, and his hair, and how his root fails to grow with his needs.

We are drawn into the brothel little by little or in an oversight. Partly because the others have already been convinced and now sleep satisfied. Partly because we forget where we are and the brilliance of the believers corners us with demonstrations of power and knowledge. Because we're lazy, and because our faith diminishes daily. Because it's probable or improbable that we will be promoted to a more respectable or at least humanly celestial hierarchy. And because after all we are no better than what we take or leave, and it's always rough going getting used to the habits we'll have to live with.
There beneath our teeming solitude we stuff innocence with

flesh, we stuff what we are and love with living death, we stuff ourselves with evasive feelings.

Faced with the desire to immobilize the fleeing beloved, you put your best words and best nights on the table; you officiate love over the bodies; you are burgeoning with possibilities, only to return to the starting point after sketching out the future. You entrust your thoughts and mistakes to emptiness, you move on, you think.
You observe, you sense the different smell of the emerging being.
You learn her name and mutter it during afternoons which have no meaning beyond the moment in which they are consumed.
You linger over what you've acquired, and contemplate her, and penetrate her, and live with her beneath the fire in which she crepitates, yields, moans, giving in to our flesh or to more remote, more inscrutable qualities.
Afterwards we become regulars. The brothel is our sun, our street for meetings, our doubting, our strange loss.
To come to this we must be very lonely, very pale under daylight and virgins' glances.
Still we must take chances, choose our next minute, stutter earthly acts and words to them, signals from simpler but more fatal galaxies, little truths to their taste that will just suffice to lose us, and hours and hours that will tunnel into us and bring us back to a confused beginning, to a slow building up towards never, towards afterwards, towards burning out.

The main part of the brothel is behind the big room. There's a hallway branching into thirty-three bedrooms, into

thirty-three bodies opening and closing in ruddy florescence.
Into beds, where skins' flavors are smoothly traded and
where jaded women lie facing the sky, while green and blue
bulbs sometimes flicker; where the women are dreamed and
felt by men of another stock, of another space; where they
are entered and everything turns round in crazy spirals of
heat and penumbra; where one experience can color an
entire past, and the queen's gambit shows the way and
scintillates.

Three shadows wait on the couples during the comings and
goings of emotion. Three lesbians are in charge of the clean
sheets and strip off the wet ones. Rosa collects the bridal
chamber dues, the wedlock tax, at the front door. Alma doles
out the empty rooms. Carla leads the couples to the door
with a dubious smile and, muttering something about a
happy marriage, shuts them in.
All three have chiseled nails and their abbreviated busts are
almost absences.
They enjoy themselves, indifferent to gossip that they've
been seen spying on the bodies making love. When I first
saw them watching with the darkness someone (now I know
who) covered my eyes.

Beyond the hallway there are quivering breasts and arms
and beds. There are fat bellies and narrow passages. There's
combustion and conflagration and slow toasting. Trembling
hands and restless eyes whose touch makes the ear they
alight on shudder.
You can hear words passing their bounds, gestures advancing
on a tightrope. Wooing, contempt and sighs.
Dread can also be heard. A sudden palpitation: what you're

touching is not real. The silky hair and the innermost part. Every fear is wary, and beneath the reddish light is not of our world but is in this world.

Persephone gets off the man's lap, without looking at where she's getting up from. The penumbra tints her face, raises and lowers it in three diverse, momentary expressions. She is standing up. Immobile. Apparently inertia weaves a secrecy in her look even more secret than she usually projects.
Suddenly aroused the music overflows in a wave of jumbled instruments.
Across the room someone mentions her name. Not calling to her, just complaining in her syllables. She neither listens nor sees. She runs her right hand through her hair. The other hand rests twitching on her stomach.
Something unsaid trembles on her lips.
She returns serenely to the man's lap.

The person who sits down is different and yet the same. The person who welcomes and embraces her is different and yet the same. Those who laugh, who kiss, who paw each other with sticky diligence are different.
They do not exist. They are there as a fragment of the vast spectacle of the brothel. They don't know that at the nearest and most distant tables others laugh and kiss and paw each other; that in many bedrooms in this place their caresses are carried out and fulfilled despite what they promise each other in private.
Just the same this passionate hoisting up doesn't save anyone from their own dangers and never saved anyone from future malice.

. . .

Persephone and the man go off in search of a bed. They
walk like zombies, holding hands. They foresee blind knots,
Gordian knots at the threshold of copulation's dwelling.
She's put her shoes on.

They disappear from my sight.
Doorless images pierce the walls. A screeching of doors blurs
the vision.
A little whore who yawns and stares at me usurps her place.
Tied shoelaces. Wristwatches. The distance from one head to
another. A zealous hand under a skirt distracts my attention.
The music makes noise. The door through which they left
unfurls a sheaf of light, casts out an emptiness I suffer
somewhere.

I observe noses, necks, feet, cheeks and damp hair. Men
who rub their arms together, massage their shaven beards. I
count one, two, three giggles from the grocer as he lifts up
Maria's dress and comments on her striped sweater.
I follow the ascent of aging Susi's tongue up the hairy chest
of a drunken mountain climber. My thoughts are those of
that priest whose tonsure wiggles as he says goodnight to a
young blonde. I notice the drops of cologne he put behind
his ears.
I hear night's darkness in the street. I feel its heavy vault
like a shell over my darkness.
I can hear inside me the regular, colorless, reedy rhythm.

Erotic filigree flies about and alights on the red carpet.
Anonymous nights and remembered nights graze against this
time of waiting, lodge in this series of arms.

Slowly and solemnly they file by, skulled-in brains, working livers, working kidneys and genitals; shadows that slacken here and there.

Euphorias and posturings, white knees, profiles go by. Trays and bottles of wine. Words that leave no trace, that neither penetrate nor absolve, that emerge like stillborn gestures.

Nostalgia for the unspoken, omens of what will be said one day.

Prostitutes talk among themselves. They compare and joke about the customers, the cut and color of their own dresses.

At times the darkness recedes like a wounded body to where cigarettes are lit, to where matches reveal chunks of yellowish flesh.

A client brandishes a cardboard sword, a nurse sitting alone at a table hums.

Some of the customers seem to be asleep talking and yawning. They stroke a young girl's breast as if it were the back of a chair. Colored fish swimming in a fog. They drink. They eat. They fornicate.

They see themselves in each other without recognizing their own image, like unsilvered mirrors. Occasionally, looking for a laugh, they blurt out a sentence or two, but so far removed from what's really happening that someone whose back was turned or who was in another room might have spoken.

The ones who are under a strain manage it impersonally, as if it were something bothersome on a lapel, a pimple on the cheek, or mud on the sole of a shoe.

Inside the gilded glass Persephone left behind I see a few wine-spotted shapes; a girl's face is an almost hidden oval;

green and slanty eyes stare out, capable of freezing time in
your smile.
The musicians take a break. They lay down their instruments
on the seats. Suddenly insignificant, they watch the
customers. The owner walks by, he nods at them. They smile
and answer effusively but the phantom doesn't listen.

Beyond the main room night moans in dual time, a knotted
simultaneous present that fades away struggling, leaving no
issue, no creation. Night and the future moan in the
exertions of the copulaters, who hold back orgasm until they
swoon, as if, panting and caught in a painful spiral, they
were training for a paradise of physical endurance.

Imagination and memory try to conjure up Persephone's
movements, the room where she lies, the man gyrating inside
her and flooding her with millions of doomed children.
But the recollection of our nakedness can't recreate this act
of love. Their bodies and faces blur into others of no
importance which, although real and close to me, can be
omitted, can fall away one by one.
Absence only resounds with departed things and beings.
There's only a whiff of a murmur. Only the silence in the
palm of my hand vibrates. The rest is drowning.

That's how Linda the Yankee forsook her English for the
sterile vocabulary that embitters all it touches.
She lost her real name in this place.
She dreamed of subterranean spaces that were not there nor
anywhere.
Of caresses fluid and lengthy as rivers.

Of winged figures who perished under the point of a
misstuck pin.
In the shadows she imagined perversions and bonfires,
lascivious cobwebs that could never be.
She languished, became thin.
She had no defenses against the animal sadness pursuing
her.
She lost her grasp on good manners.
Gone were her green skirt and her love of surprises.
Her gestures became vague, her laughter disarticulated and
gratuitous.
Her mind was sinking into lakes of silence.
Her acts no longer coincided with what she thought she was
doing.
Her face fled every lighted place, her skin fled every
touch.
She lived in corners, where there was nobody.
Her poignant blue eyes gazed at me in bewilderment as we
went off together down the short staircase.
As she saw it, she was flying down to a level where there are
no words.
On the night she went away, just before leaving, standing
gray and ashen in the doorway, she blasphemed before all
and insisted frenetically that God was vile and the world
made up of imbeciles and prostitutes.

To get into the brothel you need a countersign or a verbal
recommendation from an important customer.
A bouncer sizes up the clients at the entrance. He estimates
their spending power.
After a brief scrutiny he nods at those worthy of admission.
His assistant opens the door for them with the surliness of a

middleman between distant desire and desire obtainable only
through him.
The chosen cross the threshold. They climb up seven steps.
Black curtains are parted.
Another flunky introduces women to them.
The inadmissible and the rejected linger outside in the
street, blowing smoke rings.
They pace back and forth, hands in their pockets, eyes
opaque.
They rehash their situation again and again. Talk among
themselves. Smile at those who enter.
They look in at the windows. Watch for the moment when
the black curtains swing aside.
They read and reread the discreet sign identifying the
brothel.
They spend hours there, their hopes wearied, in the certainty
that a merrymaking—or even a confusion—following its own
laws is taking place inside without them.
They listen to the music, the shouts, the words with an
almost pious devotion, as if they had been barred from a
ritual.
The night sky that rises and falls above their heads, now
ignoring them, now oppressing them, seems to tint their
faces with its black substance, to tear at their clothes with
gusts of wind.
The distant striking of a clock periodically reminds them
that the party is going on, that an hour has passed.

The watchdogs at the door weren't so strict the first few
months, they didn't inspect each man or intimidate the
customers.
Any face was welcome, any soul in pants.

The owner smiled, the waiters patted our backs, wished us a
good evening, lead us to the tables.
The deference shown to the inquisitive was excessive, even
annoying, since it was unanswerable.
Agreements were reached without haste, effortlessly,
spontaneously.
Night followed night with its schedule of pleasures. We felt,
without knowing it, that this was gaiety.

But enemies of the adolescent trade, of suggestive come-ons,
of refinement and mercantilism in private relationships,
assailed the secret nights. Judicial rats, legalistic rats,
inspectors of decency, watchmen of God, fathers' sons with
their hearts in order, sons of mothers in saintly
menstruation, respectable defenders of respectability imposed
their sacred thistle, their blessed thorn, their dry land, their
holy water.
They forced the stability of their kind of love upon this
inconstancy of shadows, upon this disoriented clock, upon
this blind time with no future or past.
And the brothel had to retrench its expansionist schemes.
And the brothel had to camouflage itself to stay alive. And
the street campaigns handing out charms, packs of cigarettes,
souvenir glasses and cards bearing the brothel's logo had to
be stopped.
Its tables were clad in yellow Formica and its customers in
spurious bonhomie, its waiters disguised as acquiescent
foxes, its whores as undefiled virgins.
Its bulk swelled beneath the twinkling stars like a dark and
solitary stain.
Its battlements spread like flammable fog. From a distance
its walls took on a human face, resembling the faces lost by

gradually assimilated, gradually ravaged prostitutes and customers.

Slowly the brothel was encircled at ground level by a ring of mud and stones.

There are wretched hovels fifty yards away. Stunted wildflowers peek out here and there between the houses. Freestanding walls, unsheltered rooms offer up familial scenes and domestic utensils to the eyes of the indiscreet. Bare light bulbs dimly illuminate an old man, a pregnant woman, a drunkard, a ragged child. Cots scarcely wide enough for half a body are the hard bed, the night's sleep for many bodies. Shards of mirrors hung from nails by coarse twine reflect fragments of impassive faces. Windows too large or too unsuitable for the walls in which they are mounted expose their unfinished wood, their hurried acquisition. Splintered lampposts like rough-hewn logs hastily thrust into the earth say a public goodnight. An inheritance of mud from past rains serves as the uncertain ground for those who walk. Scatology, fornication, midwifery can be had for a wink, a cigarette, a coin. Solitary men lurch along the streets, or hesitate at the threshold of their houses, doubting whether to go out or stay home. Shabby old men rest placidly on cement benches, their eyes open even in sleep. An occasional beggar, with the face of a survivor, leans against a wall talking to himself, his arm outstretched as if in a splint.

Grim, drugged-looking policemen extort money from hookers, hoodlums, paupers and uncouth boys who surreptitiously slip cards to passersby advertising a sister or a mother, or roughhouse in aimless gangs, or peddle trinkets and dirty pictures.

The shacks cluster in a single line curving around the brothel, a river that circumscribes but touches neither it nor the ground where the building looms amid noise of prosperity and celebration.

The customers are well aware that this conglomeration of squalor ringed the brothel until it became a compact belt, a part of the inner atmosphere; its inhabitants perhaps fancying that this haven would become an ever-deepening source of revenue and that some of the abundance would reach its outskirts.

And so at night, and even during the day, you can see paltry dives opening for business, luckless streetwalkers offering themselves to the first comer, to the first pair of pants, the first shirt, women of ambiguous sexuality who have come from distant parts of the city or from the brothel itself, old men and sex maniacs making love in the street to budding prepubescents and teenagers.

And sometimes daybreak reveals the bloody bodies of men and women who lost their lives and divine breath in the climax and rituals of drugs and copulation.

Soon dawn will light up a bird's or a man's corpse within this belt of misery.
Torn dresses and underwear will greet the day that undoes the shadows.
Shoes belonging to a stranger, or to a no longer acknowledged acquaintance, will gleam in the sunlight.

Day will arise, take over the sky, explain the night, disjoint anecdotes and incidents.
But now a bus station bulks on the horizon, and a tin roof reflects the last glint of a far-off night.

Darkness has declined, keeps declining. A wind of heavy feathers drifts in slow motion, swathes and unswathes with dragging difficulty. Here and there it shows a dark eye, a chair leg, a red thigh. Withered milked-dry breasts shudder at its touch.
Whatever it uncovers that doesn't tremble seems not to be alive.

Can you hear? Can you understand? Do you get it? There's a music reserved just for you. There's the dust you were promised.
You can use any fire. Except caustic. Except will-o'-the-wisp. Except fireball. Except a few others. Use them all.
There's wood in the brothel. Stripped wood and split wood. Branching antlers. There's sopping fog and squalls to quench your fires. There are dead leaves to feed your flames. Knees, socks, ties. Clinging vines, pruned and untrimmed.
There are words, murmurs burning inside themselves.
You have waning hours and wasted hours. You have mouths for laughter and mouths for truths.
You have astral time and mean time, and paschal time to ponder over what doesn't blaze up.
You jump from egg-white eye to twisted eye. You seek a sign, a secret, a revelation at each jump.
We descend amid music and dust.
Amid fires and more fires. Amid wood and fog. Amid leaves and wind.

. . .

And where would we like to settle down?
There's a corner. A face is there. Here's a coat. Hands.
There are heights, depths, plenitudes in each instant.
Some customers rest their heads on their folded arms.
Others pull in their legs, still others lounge standing up.
The alert ones comb their hair, rub their eyes.
Susi is humming at the window, her hair unkempt.
Looking into a mirror, Alma takes off her painted face.
Pregnant girls go by with an air of artless vacuity. Their
breasts are scantily covered by scarves or blouses. They
shake their handbags, smiling with no smile.
A general goes by, bumping into tables, one hand held high
in salute. Befuddled by the music, he tries to brush noisy
cobwebs from his ears. The copper gilt medals have lost
their luster. His uniform has only one button and one
pocket. He suddenly takes a false step and kisses the floor.
He crawls along slowly, as if behind a parapet or slithering
through a tunnel. He says rosebay for bay leaf. Flurry for
fluster. And laughs happily.
Drunkards piss on the sly.
The musicians bleat a sugary tune.
Bodies press against each other and separate. Mutual
caresses meet. A night owl sings, leaning on his elbow.
Some watch. Others dance.
Everything seems to be moving in place. No immobility, no
movement is out of place.
Inside the turmoil, everything sleeps.

And in which instant will we remain forever?
Which statue of salt will be our statue?

Which expression will prevail, will shine on our ruined
faces?
What dust or plant will issue from our fingers like a
posthumous offering?
In whose memory will our terror repose, like a brittle,
blurred tablet?
What unsatisfied fury of love will beat its butterfly wings
now and then over our corpse?
And in which instant do we really live?
Behind which eyes do we watch, are we seen, do we pass by,
are we provisional guests, God's imaginative animals?
Which sky is this, nearer and more distant; which abyss is
this, shallower and deeper?
Which unspoken language, which shapes that are not ours,
which memories, which nights will disappear forever?
Those dark clouds are breaking up over there. Those bodies
which were us are decaying there. Those rambling dreams,
those dreams which were us, are mingled there.
Depth falls into depths, words fall into the voice.
Light elsewhere lowers its weightless birds.
Light elsewhere is light of our light.
Somewhere in God this ascent of the heights is
accomplished.
Radiance is accomplished.
Tomorrow when we awake there will be roots from that
ground in our roots; unamazed we will see colored sounds
reverberating soundlessly.
Elsewhere day foretells our arrival. But that is not our day.
Soon the sun's blazing lantern will light up the night. Twelve
livid hours will strike noon. But that is not our day.

· · ·

Even though there's a rooster at the pinnacle of our loyalty
and a windblown wildflower at the crest of our flight.
And buried in the surface, we move along a horizontal abyss.
And disguised in colors that explode at dusk, we are
polychromed where the wasteland discharges its sting of clay.
We provide for our masks, we endow them with names and
mournful whispers.
Here and there we shed an aching drop of sacred matter, a
flimsy joy, a secret barely belonging to God.
Absence plucks its spaced strings at the very center where
resemblance hovers. Solitude turns on its songs. Weariness
and boredom are twin snakes peering from the eyes of the
curious, from the parted lips of those who think they are in
love, from the tremulous genitals of those who compel
themselves to desire.

Someone gives us nothing between two bodies.
Someone separates bones from our bones, embraces from our
embraces.
Emerges from within us like an unexpected visitor, the
decisive guest who came to the party before us to give us,
when we come upon him, a cool welcome and a dismayed
farewell.
Everything we did, when we thought we were alone, was to
please him.
Everything we didn't do, when we felt listless, was to annoy
him.
With pious devotion he sang of our coupling. With profound
and soaring discourse he recounted our passage.
With unearthly skill he loosed the Gordian knots which we
didn't realize were binding us.
Let us thank him.

Thank this unrelenting giver of life, this sanguine,
remembering witness.
Thank this effusive tracker of trivialities, of unspoken and
expressed sarcasms, of stupid faces beneath the full moon.
Let us ask him what he would have done, when doubting
in our doubt, he chose with us, among others, the alley
which goes around the block only to end up at the same
place.
Let us talk to him. He knows more about us than we do. He
knows what we want to ignore in spite of knowing it.
Since our end will be a tune for churches and bordellos,
altar incense and bedding for whores and pimps.
Since it will be announced by a lout who had nothing to do
with the whole business.
Since we can always be remembered at the moment when
our beloved seduces a grocer or some jackass wearing a vest.
Let us thank him. Give dazzling nights to him.

And let the crew-cut floozie come and tell us what happened
to a customer, how somewhere he met a naked woman who
suckled him at her breast, who made him kiss her backside
and her thighs, her navel and her ears, her neck and her
ankles.
Let her describe, blow by blow, his confusion, his dismissal,
how he went on his way, his stumblings, his evil thoughts,
the feelings aroused by the woman left behind, calling him
and moaning for him with eager passion.
Let her say how, as he lost sight of her, he came upon two
naked women with the same face as the woman he had just
left, and how one of them informed him that he had made
her pregnant and that she would have twins, and how the
other one was devoid of sensuality, as if she were backward

for her age or an eleven-year-old with the face of a woman
of thirty.
Let her narrate, word by word, movement by movement, how
the customer, after brushing them aside and resuming his
way, met a naked man with the same face as theirs and how
he tried to walk past him but still the man took him in his
arms and he barely had time to think: I'm done for.
And now he sings a different song.
Let her talk about that customer as if she were talking about
dresses and stockings, about whims, fancies and shoes.
Perhaps the recollection will bring color to her cheeks, lend
intensity to her soul, make her live for a while.
Afterwards she'll reassume her arms, her eyes, her lips, her
whole body.

A fleshy, wide-hipped girl walks by me.
A milky whiteness about her knees and breasts catches my eye.
Sheathed in black cloth, her back is an erect stem topped by
a black flower.
Her arms flail the air with a rower's clumsiness.
Her flimsy black skirt still sways in my gaze despite her
absence.

A dozen women dressed in red saunter in. Identical masks
cover their eyes with the selfsame wink.
Thin, and of similar build, they all smile at once.
The first one appears to be in charge. She intimates that the
others are cloned from her, slender, faithful doubles.
They look over the clientele without moving apart, silent and
lascivious.
The tights confining their round thighs reveal innumerable
soft gaps, an imprisoned pallor.

They space themselves about ten feet from the door and the
front row of yellow plastic-topped tables.
A calculated indifference, at times a chilly stupor, flutters
above their heads.
The men stare into them, seeking out what lies inside or
behind, staring as if besotted, as if hypnotized by the
incessant movement of their earrings.
Occasionally they exteriorize a sleek, frowning impatience.
They're waiting for the music to begin, with the virtual
certainty that it will begin.

And the music does begin.
And the brothel comes alive, the whores and customers come
alive, Persephone, at the bottom of her well, is alive, I am
alive.
Placid faces, ties and dresses, bare knees, socks of many
colors, pants and jackets in motion glide back and forth.
White breasts, veined, broad, opulent, handled hour after
hour, their nipples sore, are twin fruits of the passing
moment.
Wrinkled thighs, makeup and ointments, greetings that reek
of cold cream and perfume are fleshy masses of aggressive
femininity.
Oscillating buttocks that punctually tick off the passage of
time suddenly sit down and turn into quiet vases.
One of the musicians is singing. Susi laughs. A train hoots.
A black face makes a deep stain in the penumbra. Leaning
on his elbows, an elderly man with a long, flowing beard
dozes at one of the tables.
A fat woman watches. A thin woman yawns. The entire
space vibrates to the noise of the cold. My bones have
become so thin that my desires twang like strings.

Whispers, the curtain at the entrance, hands dangling from
arms weigh down the air.
Beyond the window the sky is an upside-down abyss, a
bottomless chasm.
Hands and feet, couples and words, earrings and smiles rise
to the sky, fall into the sky.
At its very bottom, a Minotaur as big as desolation bides his
time watching.

In a bed, Persephone relishes her horizontal spiral. Amorous
grooves dovetail in her groove. Tiny women take their
pleasure in her fluted sound. A crowd of Persephones hold
back at the edge; girlish Persephones float up on dreamy
wings in search of their instincts.
Most of them flock to her center. They sway with multiple
touch and suck. Swell and shrink and suck. Stretch out their
small arms in wild circles.
They drop like petals, one by one. Head in different
directions, become aromas scattered by the wind. Far away
they fall to pieces, like something polished too roughly.

She draws everything into herself, turns it around, and then
externalizes it.
She allows everything and bestows herself as if it were
another who, submitting, yielded.
With a certain astonishment and pleasure she verifies that
her alleyway is still in the same place.
With a certain ingenuousness she discovers that her arms
embrace, that her crushed body can also crush, that her
furor conceals her moaning.
She gives way to a fluid convergence where time sinks
instead of floating.

She smells and anoints herself with resemblance on sweating
necks, on necks that explore flowerings between her legs.
She blooms in herself, confronting the other who fails to
advance with the consuming rhythm.
She powders over images whose features are blurry, where
terror is more present to her than fear.
Where countless Persephones want to flee towards her,
tearing themselves away from an enforced, indivisible
company of disintegrating objects and people.
Before and behind she is shedding Persephones. Above and
below Persephones are cast off.
At each instant she sheds a face, at each step a body.
Persephones worn out years ago, abandoned at any turning,
at any corner, wait for her on a street, in a chance word.
They come to meet her and join with her, reassume her face,
her body, her bewildered expression.
They range themselves before and behind, above and
below.

Meanwhile the key turns and the telephone rings and there
are three people walking and talking;
and they talk without stopping, and sink into silence talking
and return to the surface talking;
talking about yesterday and now, about an unglazed window,
about a color that fades into another color;
talking about the next path and the next car and the next
balcony, where there's sometimes a smiling girl;
talking about skulking furniture which welcomes you
impassively, about heavy women who laugh without
laughing;
talking about the watch's hands, which should stop at nine
o'clock;

when each one must separate from himself and walk alone
towards home: there in the park.

Towards home, at the hour imposed by a shadow dressed as
a woman,
to change company, to change clothes, to catch his breath
and put on a different pair of shoes,
to step out into the street once more, arm in arm with the
shadow, and go on talking,
talking about housework and pantyhose, about beauty parlors
and warm afternoons, about strange animals on even stranger
islands, about people devoured in schools and offices,
about new movies and glossy made-up actors who pretend to
escape from the police, and get into a taxi:
get out of a taxi, walk along the street, go to their homes,
are received by a shadow who will go on and on about
housework,
about afternoons of excitation and hours of waiting that have
foundered.

Meanwhile the key turns and the telephone rings, and three
shadows are waiting;
and they talk to themselves and enumerate object after
object, worry after worry;
and they make plans while dusting a table, washing the
windows, closing the curtains;
every now and then looking out of the window, all girlish
shivers and giggles;
listening to each sound, to each voice that floats up from the
street like a distant greeting;
noticing the alarm clock, winding it up, in the dark rooms,
on the old dressers;

as if the next minute would be decisive, would justify the
whole day, if the doorbell rings and the longed-for face
appears.

If the doorbell rings and someone smiles at them in time,
offers them their time;
a monotonous time, but human after all, bringing at least a
certain warmth which they couldn't enjoy by themselves;
which they wouldn't want, even if they could;
since this is why they've wasted all morning and afternoon,
and several hours of night;
since this is what they've saved themselves for like a fancy
dress in the closet, laboriously climbing each minute;
have come and gone thinking about nothing, have been there
like fruit ripening in secret;
lying in wait for the moment, for the right touch that will
strip off their peel,
so that, modestly and with amazement, they can let their
juices flow.

Meanwhile other bodies unwind the thread, with a few
stormy variants, with a few moans foreseen only by God.
And a customer apologizes for being what he is, bald and
obese, as he tries to get the whore who's listening to him to
take off her dress and let him put it on:
he's naked, a white blotch, parading his flabbiness and
clutching it with fumbling hands.

In the main room many are only a nose, a finger, a breast, an
ear, a thigh, a garbled sentence, an empty glass, a scrap of paper.
The penumbra and the sound seeping from the walls touch
these features, these organs.

The carnival snake charmer nests here; the eagle woman
preens her wings and beak here; the bat woman drops her
black cloth like a fright from the past that issues from me to
clothe in fantasy some pathetic tarts who are neither snake
nor bat nor eagle. Blood-red and dressed in mourning, they
are dancers lost in their farce.

Three women are dancing naked; they move their sagging
bellies as if they were moving a heavy object, an ill-fitting
roundness, a partly-hatched abdominal thought, apparent now
inside, now outside.
A fortyish virgin pants, yawns and exhales breath like
smoke; she looks about with distaste, feigning boredom. An
inedible pear, she lifts her skirt and the blackness of her sex
smells of the southwest wind and other things described by
scatology.
I hear a shout: Thorns! and she awakens. Lowers her skirt
and cowers, blinded by the light of a match; she cries over
the long-gone days of her first communion.

Many are reduced to a belt, a dry throat, a hair. They whiffle
a tune of poison and grief over the mist and stone.
Others recite insomniac trivia. The memory of shoes, of
orders and shipments, of merchandise lost and recovered
keeps them from sleep.
Some take what others give without giving themselves.
Others give all they have without giving anything. Others are
neither men nor women: dressed in virility they answer
coyly, bound in girdles they are more than men. Bartenders,
tailors, shoemakers become deaf when their names are called
out, as if the poor devil who recognizes them would strip
them naked, since most of them, when they stepped into the

street, when they came into the brothel, had left their brains, hearts and teeth in a closet, had put on their senses at random and in haste, putting memory on their knees and souls in their genitals.

Many of the women are only make-up, sham facial highlights. They go to bed colorless, hairless, nude. They get up, put on a face, a wig, breasts, buttocks.
Hands, eyes, ears, mouths are moving in a corner, telling stories, listening. They become excited, stare with each other's stare, talk with each other's words, so that at times the original and the copy are indistinguishable.
Some buy mirages, others sell them.
The owner will send a good-looking whore out on the street to attract men, or a man to attract undecided boys, and almost always before the bait returns to the brothel the fish are there waiting for it.
An inner snare, a black cord moves the pendulum, the quavering hand that guides these indolent subjects of nobody to the air they breathe in and out.

Marta goes by, dyed hair, bulky breasts, deceptive buttocks, bright red lips, pasty face, bare thighs.
Clara looks like she's come from a street fair, wearing laughter in her hands and ears, a disguise on her head and feet, her bosom and legs encased.
A bearded, mustached man comes in; he stares at Rosamunda, takes two steps towards her and stops, takes three more and stops.
A customer peers out from the darkness and yawns. The instants rise and fall on his face, hide behind his glasses, bind themselves to his shoes and his immobility. They

dangle from his fingertips, swaddle him, lift him up and drop him. They stamp a patch of shadow on his cheeks, at the commissure of his whispering lips. They make him appear and disappear. The darkness that takes his place doesn't remember him.

Two or three words to the torpid doorman: I snort "open sesame" at the pest.
And the brothel door will open. And the immediate future will open. And the fountain of life will open. One second after the entrance. One second after the stair.
Beyond the curtain and the welcoming waiter. Beyond the owner, who greets us.
The first wall and its pornographic drawing has been overcome, the first whore who says good evening.
Already we are uniform and red, flushed shoulders and flushed landscape. Skeptical and worldly. With determined hands and hoarse voices. Shielding our eyes we watch.
Certain that everyone is looking at us and thinking we are merciless, capable of splendid and unusual cruelty or contempt.
Smoke, words, convincing details of acts we've never performed are whirling around our bodies. Sobbing in our future are women we will never whip, memories we never imagined. Just so our past won't be alone in the brothel.

We go up and inside without exactly wanting to go up and inside, a mechanical movement like fingers holding out a bill to buy a ticket, without consulting desire's wishes.
It's as if we had to convince ourselves of the reality of a thing which is there, which we have already seen and

known, but which memory renders unreal or makes too vivid
to accept its existence.

Because the floor we tread is scarcely human. It is said never
to have felt daylight, the infiltration of a luminous beam that
dazzles a moth at the window and stops the bat's flight like a
frozen wall.
It seems as if we were floating, such is the lethargy that
elevates so many gathered shadows, so much frivolity at
once,
that jettisoned love and sleep on the way to attain greater
lightness, more agility, swifter certainty,
when rancor, suspicion and a dagger must cut down a
conscience which may have judged them unthinkingly.

Darkness, the brothel's congenital termite, spreads over the
man in the torn shirt—of a blue fallen out of favor—and
over the beautiful women gossiping and laughing, making
plans and laughing.
It spreads over glasses and chairs, the dancer's jacket and
the sounds he hears, the exploring floozie's fingers provoking
erections in the dim closeness.
It spreads over the young girl's nose as she leans forward so
that her breasts, oranges of another hierarchy, will separate
heavily.
It spreads over Susi as she sits in a corner, covers her gaze,
her grimace, her chestnut hair, her inquiries about good and
bad weather.

The masked women dance in the gloom. White patches of
skin, polished nails, rouged cheeks are the colors, the

polychromatic stelae of a time that is fading, the chance hues
of an instant that will never return.
Resembling live, blazing pyres, they allow themselves to be
led. Supple as quicksilver that jumps when squeezed, they
bend their bodies backwards and forwards. Their partners, a
secretary, a locksmith and a cabinet minister seem foreign to
their rhythm, mere pretexts for a tripartite ritual they can't
understand and to which they are not admitted.
They have the faces of ugly birds, jackdaws and magpies.
They are surprised when the leader takes the fairest woman
in her arms and kisses her on the mouth, as if she were
repeating an habitual act.

Women whose armpits and thighs are shaven, whose hair is
dyed and whose voices are nasal gnash their teeth when they
speak, when they spit out a remark about the nearest whore.
A young deaf-mute feels he is strangling when he can only
manage to say *see* and *so* instead of the whole sentence
which is choking him.
A sleeping judge converses with a dead man done in by the
judge's diurnal sleepwalking; broken bones and twisted
words issue from his twisted mouth.
A young girl apologizes to two customers for being
indisposed; standing on the stage she argues softly, abstruse
in both her body and her reasons, half-naked and slovenly,
her expression of solitude and anger clashing with her
beauty.

A loud dialogue crosses the room:
"Yes, I love, I fuck, yes, I am Irene Parayanos . . ."
"But . . ." "You're not worth the price of a bed."
"You're worth less than an undershirt, a drink, a cigarette."

"You're not worth the trouble of having you without a bed."
"You're worth less than the trouble of picking off a scab, of
seeing you, of touching you, of talking to you . . . *But* . . .
Go away. Let's not be a train on the tracks or a lighthouse
sticking through a cloud."

But it would be inaccurate to say that there's a deeper
descent, a riper loneliness than the bemedaled colonel's, who
waves vanity into his gray hair, and who now is asking Susi
about her gold tooth and questioning a distant customer
about his early baldness, all the while hiding his nose in the
darkness to conceal a reddening cold.
Than the loneliness of the painter or the jeweller who pursue
the owner around tables and through rooms trying to sell
him a painting, a necklace, a ring, led on by greed and
goaded by effrontery. And they utter lying words and
sophisms with their eyes and ears, drowning him in cheap
prose.
Than the loneliness of the old man pretending to be thirty
who sprays spittle and sings through his molars and whose
chest trembles as he murmurs seductive words to Blanca.
Than the loneliness of the man who makes his presence felt
through mortgages, IOUs and deeds, and who, when asked
his name, ipso facto presents a credential signed by a
stranger.
Than the loneliness of three pliant innocents who falter at
each step as if missing something, as if verifying they had
left the crucial part of themselves at home and put on vests
instead.
Than the loneliness of the fat man indiscriminately gobbling
spaghetti or duck while digestion and time unravel him, keep
him forever from flight.

. . .

Relegated to the basement, dishwashers, busboys and
sluggish cooks have made a hive of domestic activity there;
coming and going beneath the main room as one multiple,
diverse body, ears solicitous, eyes attentive, receiving
messages and orders from above with malicious scowls;
as they pluck a goose's neck, plunge a chicken into boiling
water, scrub tomatoes and floors and handles, change rusty
spits holding legs of lamb and pork, and thread the remains
of small birds on skewers;
as they grease the axle of a wheel, turn dust into eggshells,
stones into bones, green blood of plants into juices, liquids
into drinks, death into a variety of flavors;
and some work slowly, others quickly; some focus on
mutilated hares, others heat water, eviscerate, skin; some
squeeze the intestines, separate them, cut two pieces from
one, four from two, and eight from four;
and others catch the blood drop by drop in a bowl, a glass, a
cup, to boil it and then throw the leavings, the unusable
minimum, into a garbage pail on which they drop the cover
as if they were sealing a tomb with a filthy stone;
there they slake lime, there they wash, there they set aside,
over yonder they sterilize, farther away they plunk down
inert red slabs, all the while squashing cockroaches, spiders,
mice and flying insects;
well provided with ovens and hearths, with frying pans,
grills, bowls, low-hanging lamps, stoves and piles of plates;
surrounded by dough, onions, egg yolks, seafood and fruit;
next to bloody pelts, dung and shattered hooves;
among fragmented, unrecognizable pigs; among eyes which
still quiver and stare; among severed, plucked, blanched
wings; among livers, hearts and brains; among vegetables,

kidneys and gizzards; among snouts and half-open beaks
about to drop forever into the garbage;
one of them crinkles potatoes, another shells peas and pours
dirty water down the drains; some hand on glasses, cups and
heaping plates until they reach a waiter standing at the top
of the stairs;
others stir up the fire (others put it out) with salamanders,
gas and illusions, content to sweat underground, since they
couldn't stand the air, would cool down too quickly, if they
were exhumed;
their faces greasy, they breathe raw meat and smells,
obedient to the knowing chef who gives the final touches, his
nose and chin meeting like a claw.

But it would be incongruous to claim that a dimension exists
which is more real than keeping one's feet amidst drownings,
than watching how an arm curls around Maria's neck as she,
aloof to the encirclement, takes a while to discover the noose
she feels choking her,
than the blind judge's, who can't sit still and keeps biting
his nails and sucking his fingers, one by one,
than Blanca, Ana and Rosamunda's complaining to the
owner about some suspicious-looking customers who are after
them,
than those two old men trying to pass themselves off as
boys, than those two boys who look like girls when they stop
laughing,
than that foursome which can only exist as a group,
than the lady and gentleman holding onto their glasses as if
the glasses were holding them up,
than those blond men pawing alike an arm, a face, a bosom
and the rim of an ashtray or the neck of a bottle,

than the men and women feeding their fires not to live
longer but to burn out more quickly,
than those who remain in the darkness gnawing at each
other, mistaking fingers and ears for morsels of food,
than kill-them-with-words and kill-them-with-silence setting
their watches as if this obsession with the right time could
make them real,
than Susi, alone on her knees, corroborating the concreteness
of a glance, of a passing figure she had dreamed,
than Magdalena suffering from the misunderstanding, the
lack of correspondence between expression and act, between
what she thinks, wants to do and does,
than being here, where honorable occupations are praised
and there's a pretense of drinking prudently.

Now that the clientele is drunk, they throw glass victims to
the floor, wrestle and hug, scratch delicate skin, pull each
other's hair and hands, lift up chairs and young girls to
prove their strength, and should they drop someone or
something, they swear on eyes and shards of glass;
they wander about like graceless angels, ponderous and
flabby, incapable of rapid movement, dull;
they call things by the wrong name, say ashtray for glass
and chair for ashtray, body for chair and table or lip for
woman's body;
they call Susi a virgin, the owner my lord of suitable
merriment, the brothel a place of good comfort, the stupid
customer personality kid, find the blasphemer droll and the
skinflint shrewd and cautious;
they describe a situation or tell a story in too much detail
and with exaggerated gestures, prodding a woman's knee or
propping their right foot against the wall; they dance

awkwardly, snorting, are carried away more by weight than
by will into busy gymnastics of kissing, knots and cuddles,
and the tallest jut out as they dance, pushing their bodies
forward like cyclists straining for balance.

Without point or purpose, between no one and nobody, out
of its profound nakedness night aims its woeful tolling at us,
its sanctified, silent schedule, its funereal love seeking and
calling to the other side of light.
Now that Susi wavers between two candidates, and a gilt
crucifix quivers against her black sweater, and her breasts
tremble and beckon;
now that Maria, with biblical reminiscences, is accepted for
rough usage by an endless and exhausting assortment of
knees, hands and organs;
now that Persephone harbors other matter inside her,
consumes other more eager coals, other weak moans in her
intense fire;
now that each waiter wears a numbered pink patch on his
back which identifies him by the table (also numbered) he
waits on, as the customers tend to confuse the waiter on the
far left with the waiter on the far right;
now that words swirl around without touching me, and trite
phrases eroded by the years congeal on my tongue.

Overcome by urgency I go to the bathroom; pensively, the
music following me.
I see feet, arms, chair legs, smoke and Susi's glance behind me,
I hear intermittent breathing, bodies creaking, footsteps
catching up with me, the screech of tables being moved.
The checkroom girl smiles at me. Her face puckers. She puts
her hands on her lap, lowers them.

A man I hadn't noticed peers out from behind her head. She
stoops, the man lunges at her. They crawl under a table and
become intertwined. Laugh gleefully. They don't come out
again.
I tap on the whitewashed walls of the corridor.
I recall a few lines by San Juan de la Cruz, a fragment of
Heraclitus, Persephone's attitude, my slow passage.
I see a squatting man amusing himself by squashing
cockroaches. He stands up when he sees me and as I pass
him bends over in an *n*, his head swinging between his legs
like a clapper.
I come upon a fat woman lifting up her dress, a servant
grabbing Magdalena's round, fruity breasts.

His elbows propped on the sink, an aging man stares at his
reflected image, poured into the mirror.
He isn't invisible. Hair, ears, neck, gesture, night, stupor, all
bear witness to his visibility.
Although the painful whiteness of the tiles, also reflected,
gathers round him, and the composite, alien noise from the
main room doesn't even reach him, and the imagined face,
and its familiar features, has a real horror.

A drowsy man, a complacent man and a cabinet minister
urinate indolently.
The latter two narrow their eyes, hold their noses.
At their side, eyes glued to the urinals, others lean forward,
the better to hear what they are doing.
Near this busy group sheets and torn shirts lie on the floor,
perforated eyes and dried bloodstains staring up at the men.
An insect falls into a glass on the sink as if into a crystalline
well.

.   .   .

I start back with a faint understanding of what this place is, of
what a man reflected in a mirror is, of what forty years leaning
on a sink means, of how little noticing these things matters.
I eliminate them, person by person, urinal by urinal, insect,
glass, eyes.
I become lighter, perhaps in order to fly, or simply to be
still: here, there, over there.
Arduously I conquer the seconds, I inhabit and think them
as if I myself were the hours devouring me, at the boundary
of spheres where merriment is normal and dread
commonplace.

I'm in the short narrow corridor, quickened by a time of
images and tracked by physical time,
a few feet away from the checkroom, from a whisper, a
rumination of a memory of a decayed concretion,
at the door of the packed main room that envelops me with
music and noise, with red lights that extend before me like
an insubstantial red carpet.
Seeing and defining myself, loath to see and define myself.
Walking along in shoes, pants, vest, and seeing that I'm
seeing myself.
I zigzag between tables, more naked in my clothes, more
naked than ever. I verify my sense of touch on the curtain, I
slide my eyes from the smoke to Jazmín. I am maladroit at
making my way through the standing talkers, at pushing
aside the knots of dancers, at clearing the obstacle of couples
leaning against the columns kissing.
The boisterous crowd is a single dancing body that opens its
arms to me, its friendly navels, its landscape of skirts, its
boring redundancy.

Impulses and rhythms, poverty and usury, tastes and smells, the ugly, the fools, the whores are recognizing each other. Not even a hair could fit between chin and blow, between breath and breath.

The childless woman has returned. She sits down, tired and blinking. Slumps in the chair. Pulls her stockings tighter. She has returned and I return. I find myself once again. I travel backwards image by image, unraveling the skein. I go from now to now, from second to second until I reach her face, until I hear her footsteps walking towards copulation. I restore her to her body. I endow her chest with blossoming breasts, I name her thighs where there was nothing. I put lips on her flesh. I speak a tongue into her mouth. I bring lids to her eyes, hair to her head. I give ten unfeeling nails to her fingers, ten cutting edges to scratch me. Looking at her I seek her. Seeking her I lose her. The wings I lend her are not mine. The air she breathes is not mine. What's over is over. Gradually I think her. I harass her with words, I dare her to come into the dream which dreams her. I tell her ghost that the world is more unreal than she is, that the dream which dreams me is also calling to her. It calls to her in the creaking of tables and the burning of time, in the blue forehead of that man who talks incessantly, in the crazy hands that spin around a circle of many clocks, in words that rise, never to return.

Persephone apologizes. Says she slept with him without any desire. Goes into detail. Stirs up the past. Launders her memory like a dress that gets dirtier when it's washed. Two customers approach her from behind and cover her

eyes, wheedle into her ears, touch a nipple and touch her neck. She laughs, to show off the even whiteness of her teeth, the innocuous sting of her tongue to an old man who is gawking at her.
When she opens her purse a tortoiseshell comb, a photograph, a pocket mirror, a coin fall out; first she picks up the comb, the mirror, the coin.
Afterwards, a long time ago, she steps on my photograph.

She has just stripped naked, shared herself, gyrated (to judge by her expression) effectively.
The clothes, the sounds, the movements she left on the couch will never be repeated.
Skilful at intimidation, at overcoming inhibitions, she lay down, she let herself be stroked and stroked in turn, admitted the admissible, ate what was edible, embraced with tangled prose.
Someone stands before her, resuscitated.

Someone throws liquid on Jazmín's hair and the dye runs; someone plucks at Rosario's bosom and wooly wisps drift to the floor.
Four white buttons stare out from a sweater, and a rampaging lumberjack fells Susi and lies on her, a cumbersome, enveloping blanket.

Under a table the same voice says *oui, yes* and *si*. Thighs spread open below, feet above.
A woman looks at me and hesitates when I look back, but she's pushed forward by the customers and whores behind her.

A clown talks to me, makes faces to get my attention, but
when I take notice of him he backs off smirking.
The owner gives advice to a waiter in a stumbling voice; the
confidant listens, his bony neck thrown back.

Now I see the self-indulgent braggart, cocky and resilient.
He hails those who brush past him as if they had spoken to
him, acknowledged him. He gives off a musty smell.
Feeling my gaze upon him, he rolls his eyes and simpers. He
has sleep in his ears, desire in his sex, eyes in his fingertips
and his soul in the cellar. Even when he stands up he's
asleep.
Squinty, blue-eyed women watch him. A vast mobile
wardrobe looks on with approval. Amidst a program of
noises, whores who are pearls threaded on the string of time
hitch onto his sonambulism.
He sweats under the color-stained tee shirt, his chin
clear-cut, eyes cloudy, arms brown and bulging. Shoes shined
and face washed. Beltless and holding a cigarette between
his fingers. Manly down to the last inch of skin, to each
organ, innards, Achilles' heel and in what doesn't show, in
what will always be distant, invisibly tormented and distant.
Brimming with answers which are really questions.
Watching us from a considerable vertigo.
Inside his head each sound has many echoes, each color
many shades.
What we think is alive is really funereal.

The music comes out of a whistle, a drum, a trumpet, out of
a melodious voice whispering a name, out of a wave that
undulates, enfolds and . . .

touches the cabinet minister's ear, the fool's hair, the
braggart's tongue and . . .
enervates them with its timely flux, chuckling and somewhat
overbearing.
The music settles reluctantly into brains, shoulders, polite
words, into salty drops on abdomens.
It rattles the windowpanes. Shakes the dust from hips, wigs
and backs. Smoothes out the years knotted up in throats,
chests, temples.
Furthers voices and scatters noises. Slowly, too quickly, it
incrusts itself, finds obedience, walls to echo it. (Echoes that
thin out, disappear, turn into other voices:
turn into song again, in smaller creatures who pursue the
escaping echo which becomes inaudible and is a song once
more in a lesser, more private space.)

Near me Magdalena cries out, her cry so subdued she could
be far away. One eye is open, the other shut. Half her body
is dressed, half is naked.
She looks young from behind, and old from in front.
Maria is missing an arm, a knee, part of her head; Susi
lacks a shoulder, an eyebrow, her lower lip, her neck: both
are immersed in shadow, dismembered by movement.

Phantoms dance toward me. They come from all sides,
big-bellied and grinning. They snap their heels, their fingers
and their teeth. A green-eyed girl goes by. A man with
heavy arms. A fat woman rowing against the current.
Here comes the floozie, becoming smaller with each step,
like a figure that, instead of drawing nearer, loses itself in
the distance until it vanishes into the ground.

. . .

Maria wears a red tie, a red blouse in the penumbra, big
black shoes to slash through the air, laughter in her body,
speed in her hands.
Susi moves like baffled clockwork. They've given her music
and she hangs onto it. They've given her a blond and she
hangs onto him.
Margarita and Blanca clasp and unclasp, entwine and
disentwine their legs; extremely similar, their flesh quivers in
easy gestures.
Margarita burgeons like a branch from an alien tree;
her head, breasts and waist appear between Blanca's long
legs.

The customers dance and the whores dance. Their whole
bodies move as they leap. They chase each other, climb over
one another, fall in line, commingle.
They're scraps of paper, motley cutouts blown about by a
musical wind.
The clients emerge from the whores, and from other whores,
still more clients: wound up, fully dressed for the brothel,
for the music.
They exude a chilly warmth. Are amazed to find themselves
moving. Eyes hear the sound. Ears see the sound.
A musician, all beard and mustache, squawks.
A pair of glasses looks sideways.
Carmen squatting over yonder.
Susi there.
Marta here.
Even with my eyes closed I can see them, I can follow them
and feel their presence.
Susi lifts a finger. Aims at my heart.

Carmen wiggles her behind, leans against a table, bends over
and offers her ass to everyone.
I open my eyes. Susi clambers onto a shadow's shoulders.
Aims at my heart.

A musician inflates and deflates his cheeks. The trumpet is
cold. He sweats, overheated by his effort.
A girl unbuttons her blouse, the rear buttons of her skirt. A
boy examines her.
The owner stares.
The waiters serve.

A finger, a hand, an arm, a nose, a chest, a head, trousers,
shoes, a jacket, shoulders, a man appear.
The cuckolded husband, the deceived boyfriend, the youthful
swindler, the beguiling woman, the tailor, the barber, the
policeman,
the inventor, the visionary and the dreamer, servants' and
whores' favorites,
are all the same foot-tapping body, the same wave cresting
and ebbing, the same noisy, suffering yawn.

The tallest stick out, arch over, disappear among the
shortest, grow again, groan and stumble giddily.
A midget dances between a tall man's bowlegs; his partner
Marta awaits him on the other side, takes his hands, lifts
him to her breast, sets him on the floor again:
midget, old child, spins like a top, opaque eyes, blond
wig, cosmetics running off his forehead, his cheeks, his
eyelids.

· · ·

The big heads of the short people jiggle at the same level,
separate and converge, cut through the air swiftly, collide,
recover, go on dancing.
Something frenetic, something minimal, a vertiginous
medianness emanates from them, from their short arms, their
chubby hands, their paunchy agility.
Next to the midget they're giants, midgets next to the tall
people. They clasp the womens' waists in a mannered way,
twirl them around elegantly, on tiptoe.
Blotches of mustache and beard protrude from their faces,
covering half their expression. The ones wearing glasses are
reduced to shadow and pain.
Little shoes, enormous compared to the midget's child-sized
shoes, intersect and disengage, are raised as if to play
football.
And in their midst Marta laughs, and the midget laughs.

The floozie dances by herself. She embraces the columns,
follows the more lively couples. Thanks the nearest man, the
closest woman for having kept her company a moment.
She lifts her skirt. Shows a bit of thigh, a brevity, a
leanness.
She rubs her fingers over her teeth, behind her ears; she
hums.
She amuses herself. Sighs to herself.
Head hanging low like a speed skater, she swiftly steps in
and out, touching bodies, until the final g of the zigzag.

The wide-hipped girl lets herself be led. The soft flopping of
her breasts gleams in the penumbra, the reddened knot of
her elbows.
She doesn't look at the man whose sinuous hands encompass

her. The excessive waistline is another matter. What is hers,
inherited, really hers, is the dark gaze, the mane of black
hair.
Too remote to be effaced by those who cover her.
She knows nothing of desire.

One of the masked women imitates the sounds she hears and
the ubiquitous tune, as she sways and runs her hand through
her hair.
A rutting mare, a slender block of ice, warm for others but
not for herself, she seems to be split in two: fire from the
waist down, straight lines above.
Growing more sensual by the minute, more labile and
smiling, her mask redder, flame is her nest, the flash of her
eyes is stony gray.

Outside night strikes the hour on street clocks, paints black
the number clearly striking.
Imprisoned within a golden ring, night is a black bird
pointing a restless hand at time, dark, warm or cold, damp
or dry.
Mother substance that surfaces from the deep covered with
unseeing eyes. Dark fallen fruit.
Night outside is a siren lure to shadows, an open wound,
almost tangible.
It wanders like dogs in search of their masters,
of the invisible canine lord who put them on trial in this
valley of bleary eyes and blows,
scans the vague horizon, tracks smells, tastes; pauses;
hears barking that warns of an enemy presence, a relay of
alarms,

hears the fatal portent of something that will compact us,
that will file down what was superfluous and profound.

The dresses change places, float or glide, eddy or drag on
the floor, go out or come on to the sound of unfolding cloth.
With a flower in the pattern, a house, a Chinaman, a tree
planted in silk, a green girl's face or a gold leaf.
Blue and yellow, black and orange, red and sleeveless, velvet
and gray. Lightweight portable houses, warm shelters.

The musicians strut, pulsate in each instrument, each note.
They urge on the most enthusiastic or impetuous couples
with euphoric phrasing, with onomatopoeic surprises.
They step down from the stage. Wander here, wander there.
Sing part of the song to an entwined pair who breathe
anxiously, with time in their guts.
Young and old applaud them, laugh in their faces. They
repeat a name in the melody every three words, like a knot
in a rope from which many people are hanging.

Thoughts buzz, fantasies, beds made ready, betrayed love,
what we never dreamed of but still happened to us.
The glance, the hallway, the checkroom, the tables of the
law, the masked women, the Face of Faces.
Silence nests elsewhere. It stares out of the antipode's
eyes, out of the luminous tokens of divinity. Ferns are its
fragrant green hands. It materializes suddenly in a river's
waters.

Focused white moonbeams come in through the window, fall
on Persephone, brightening her. Touch her feet, thighs and
lips. Encircle her neck. Shine on her forehead with an air of

worship, an air of concealing something that can be told to
no one. Fall like beams that are signs, signs that are omens.
Alongside the stars whose inner radiance is such that we feel
illuminated, as if darkness had opened up eyes inside us, is
the star who presides over the dawn, who renews her form,
who is cool as crystal, a pearl cast on black cloth.
Created to shine in the dark, she only reveals a part of her
light. Sun's mirror, alone in the gloom, wherever she looks
she sees God's face.
Today she glitters with a brilliancy like the one in which
God made the archangel Gabriel dip his wing. A golden
fringe on her halo is a reminder of that day.
Today she has shells and fishes in her waters.
Today a hare courses through her spots.
Breath dwells in her, habit carries her forward.
But here below, where earth and sky merge in the
uniformity of darkness, Persephone looks at me with
unremembering eyes, moves her lips soundlessly, as if
talking in her sleep.
The blood seems to have left her cheeks and ears to rush
towards, to catch on fire in a part of her body which is not
visible.
Her jittery hands drum an annoying, repetitive rhythm on
the table, her anxiety is so overwhelming it's as if the
sounds and the table were weighing on her heart.
An unfamiliar face usurps her features. She loses one color,
acquires another, fixes her eyes on my uppermost vest
button.
She wrinkles her forehead, a few hairs fall as she abruptly
raises her head, still looking downwards nearsightedly in the
direction her chin points.
The words she speaks are more like grunts or sighs.

There she sits, pregnant with something, round with
misgivings. Waving her hands in my face.
She looks out the window slowly. She lingers over old
furniture, mounds of sand, women's clothes.
She pauses at spots on the windowpane, at the customers'
faces, and then looks at me with an excess of affection
seeking where to take hold.
The drumming continues, at odds with the rhythm
undulating through the room.
The window reflects blurry figures and objects, reflects what's
happening inside.
Out in the street trees rise up like dark towers.

Persephone drinks up the wine in both glasses, so
lackadaisically that it's hard to say she is drinking.
Persephone stands up, her features transformed, and sighs,
and her foot trembles behind her, as if it were listening.
Several drunks are sleeping, their mouths open wide, their
dreams open wide, their glasses still on. White shirts gleam
in the darkness like newsprint. Women pat each other's
backs, twist their curls; they seem to have lost their tongues,
and talk in gestures.
Broad shoulders are pillows to recline against, sagging
breasts are bunched shoulders to lie on.
Susi kisses me surreptitiously with two fat, salty lips. She
licks my neck. Slobbers on my cheeks. I let her sing into my
ear, tell me something about Persephone.
Some sleep in profile, noses aiming footwards. Their ties are
pendulums.
There are red lights here, people sitting there.
An old man's bristling gray hairs point to the ceiling.

A dirty page from a comic book is trampled. An insect is trampled.

"Is that man's name Esquirio or Escarro?" asks a voice in the penumbra.

Magdalena fumbles in her purse. Takes out a roll of Life Savers. Offers one to Susi, one to Maria. Returns it to her purse. Puts on a sweater. She's cold.

The floozie is singing. An old man coughs. Bespectacled Marta fidgets and turns around, giggles with a young man who puts his feet on the table.

Maria scratches at something stuck to her thighs. Susi stares at her own knees. Candida unbuttons her coat, buttons it, rubs her behind, stands up, walks off.

I light a cigarette. Susi leans over for a light as well. Maricarmen joins us. I'm about to burn my fingers. I throw the match on the floor, while they snicker.

The midget seeks his spurious mother, points to her as if he were choosing a toy, rapidly says:

"Daddy doesn't know where you left his new vest."

Magdalena puts on a pair of glasses. A customer calls a waiter, hissing *beeeeeaaaaassssssst-beeeeeeaaaaassssssst.* A girl takes off her shoe. Carmen crosses her legs. Rosario uncrosses hers. Luisa, chin in hand: "Did you call me?"

"Almost," the midget and I answer simultaneously.

Makeup melts like a wax mask off a middle-aged woman's face, and a violent red glares from her lips.

Angelica receives a man in public, just like a bitch welcoming the first dog who mounts her.

The wide-hipped girl's breasts are as big as if she'd already given birth.

The floozie peers over the shoulders of two men with pointy
heads, a moon between two pine trees.
Thin men seem heavy, short men tall.
A clock strikes five.

Persephone and a customer stare at each other. Marta smiles
at a shadow on the wall. A policeman rifles a drunk's
pockets, like a vulture scavenging a corpse's brains.
There are some people who sleep while they talk and wake
up talking. They call the whores ladies and the brothel a
place for coupling.
Persephone goes up one step, but there's still another. With
obvious coquetry she lets herself be considered admirable.
She is armed with embraceable buttocks, breasts, thighs and
arms.
She wears golden crescents in her ears, and what she hopes
to be, in her lapis lazuli night.
Laughter issues from her mouth and other parts of her body.
She is already on the chessboard.

Susi sits down at a table to talk with the floozie. The floozie
is playing with a flower in her hands.
Susi scrutinizes the darkness like a hare who sees clearly.
She spots a waiter. Says his name. He is with her. Their
three faces are rumpled by the frequency of obsequious
grimacing, of ear-to-ear smiles. Susi and the tart order
between jokes. The waiter is off on winged feet.
They whisper, share secrets, look around myopically, put
their elbows on the table, wait.
Every dog barks at them, every bird winks at them.
They eat together, drink together, go home together when

they're thrown out of the brothel, together they became
whores, together.
Whores at the threshold, in bed, on the street, sitting at a
table, and also when they pray.
They frown everywhere, look inside each sound to see if
someone is searching for them.
They eat off their backsides, drink off their breasts, are giver
and receiver.
The penumbra turns their hands purple, their faces are the
same face and they grow by sinking.

Persephone is siren or fairy, hot and cold, damp and dry;
blackened, whitened, red.
The colors of her body change. Her moonstruck being
irradiates light out of both eyes.
The dancers and others who are awake watch her as she
goes by, observe her hips, measure the abundance of her
breasts, stare at me passing among them.
They don't matter to themselves, they are branded by
gluttony, by the raw reality which does match the raw dream
they had.

Swathed in penumbra we cross the room.
Tables, chairs, voices are left behind calling to her and
calling to me.
She parts the curtains first, then I do.
We descend step by step. Our footsteps are barely audible,
they scarcely touch the floor, the stairs.
There's smoke coming out of my mouth. There's a head
which doesn't look back to see if I'm following. There's a
body walking alone.

I am alive in the customers' suspicions, I enter into their
remarks, they fight over me. I go out to separation and the
street. I feel cold. I see night, a silent vault. Moon and stars,
we're not alone in the night.
In the street now. Three young men speak to her. Turned
down by the brothel, they were keeping vigil to see what the
brothel might throw into their arms as a consolation prize.
I'm cold.

Persephone comes back without looking at them, without
looking at me. Walls, windows on which dew petrifies pass
by her side, she leaves them behind.
She hasn't seen me, doesn't see me.
We reenter the brothel, the voices, the high-pitched waves of
the cymbals.
She's still in front, I'm still following her. I try to remain
alert, to pinpoint exactly what shouldn't fool me.
I add a detail to the customers' predictable faces. I undo
their expressions. She and I receive in silence greetings from
Susi, Maria and Magdalena, watching us return.

Once again on the chessboard, among the imperfectly drawn
pieces of my color and size.
On the neutral square, like a green squire, always loitering
at the queen's right hand, advising her in her chess games;
almost a live pawn, an extra substitute pawn, dropping from
one slander to the next, a dart constantly piercing my sex,
more concerned with my own hands, my feet, my chest than
with what's going on around me.
Surrounded by creatures lacking vituperation or praise, by
shadows that neither flash nor fade, that neither feel
affection nor destroy, that neither descend from nor rise

above that unilateral limbo where they slowly shrink and
disappear.

When they're tired they become like blind animals, like dogs
lolling in the sun and the night; they fling themselves down
anywhere, heed no one, no longer even try to show the
courtesy they feigned.
They lie in a familiar place, in a strange place, where they're
put, wherever they fell, wherever they're left.
And wherever they are they disparage each other, eat and
drink when they can, acquire bodies, objects and noises to
shore themselves up. They talk when they feel lonely, and
sleep in the interstices.
They are neither inside nor outside, neither sitting on the
chairs nor standing at the door. They sail in a fog through
indistinguishable days.
The minute they die they will realize that they haven't been
here or anywhere, that they didn't endure one or two weeks
of unreal holidays, but many years of tedious reality.

The red lights receive our steps. A waiter's fervent eyes
welcome us. Owls and bats, eyeglasses and matches observe
us.
Susi is creeping. Beneath her a man drags them both across
the room. Susi frees her breasts and their flaccid exuberance
spills out with a categorical plop.
The sounds of the song being played break into bits. A
laugh slips between the notes, flaps against the air as if
someone were breathing avidly, their throat turned inside
out.
From the stage the owner acknowledges an anonymous
civility, because, excepting myself, no one is looking at him.

.   .   .

Persephone leans against a column humming. She puts her
foot on the chair, turns her face toward the wall. Gnaws on a
piece of bread in the corner. Drinks beer with two men.
Passes from red light to darkness and becomes night.
A small flame darts from her eyes. Her face is a question
mark, a walking suspicion. When they call her "whore" she
smiles, when they feel her up she winks obscenely.
Bird that lays golden eggs, she will soon find someone to
dismember her prospecting for veins of gold in her innards,
to add another groaning recollection to her memory.
But now, a lonely obese man summons her, an obese man
who has one red leg, half a red stomach, chest, head, and
the rest of his body is black.
As Persephone comes closer he laughs with half a mouth,
puffing out one eye and a cheek. He welcomes her with
red-black fingers, perhaps with half-words as well.

Standing here, my hands empty, squinting like a mourner
who draws the curtains against the light, or someone who
discovers his invisibility, his inefficacy, in the middle of a
crowd.
Solemn and withdrawn, I stealthily observe what the others
are doing, how they stammer, what they aren't doing, could
do and leave off doing.
I measure the distance Persephone's glances travel, the lack
of coherence between what she says and what she thinks.
I put my hands on the table, my elbows, my chin on my
hands, words on my chin.
I dream of Mr. Bones, Mr. Pink, Sargent On and Sargent
Off, the Honorable Banal Balance, Mrs. More and Mr.
Foreskin. They're gathered together, slapping each other on

the back, waiting on their own tables; when I join them
and then leave they hail me with an almost martial
barking.
I dream of the young tarts' bastions, stormed by the
customers. Who could count those jumbled breasts?
I long to find in the outside world the interior reality
that sustains us, undermines us and destroys us. It's as
if I were listening to someone arguing, and the more he
waves his arms about, becomes excited and gesticulates, the
less it matters what he's saying, and the more indifferent
the listener becomes. I'm like a man circling a stationary
object who didn't realize he was being watched and, like
someone who can't sleep during the day—but has slept—
suddenly awoke because his dreams were troubled and
he feels he is falling into the midst of those who are not
sleeping.
I see walls, chair backs, hearts which a ray of daylight will
never reach.
I see the window. I see within myself what will never be
repeated.
Secretive lights play. Silent songs are heard.
I see women who tug at their necklines, display the spot
where they throb, lower their arms, tilt their glances.
I see bodies fall and get up, feet stretch out and walk,
mouths pucker and unpucker, fingers like pennants on huge
breasts, stallions trampling mares underfoot.
I remember how St. Jerome held a newborn baby in his
arms and thought it was a boy, since the parents had given
him the girl well swaddled.
I remember that when St. Jerome gave the baby—now
touched with saintliness—back to them, the parents arrived
home to discover that the girl had turned into a boy.

. . .

I remember that when he entered her, she said, "I'm
breaking. My body is breaking apart. Half is going south,
half is going north. God is to the north and to the south. My
bones are glass. My glass is colored. I can feel the red bone
go by saying, 'Now you've severed me.' And the white bone
saying, 'Don't go too far away, I'll be with you until you
die.' My flesh is the flesh you see at the butcher's, still
warm, its fibers and nerves sheathing a femur. And now that
I think of it, that's all I am, a little less and somewhat more
than a sheath."
Afterwards she pushed him aside. Got out of bed, walked
around naked. Lit a cigarette and began to dress, blowing
out the smoke as if her soul went with it.
Not one smile did she have, not a single word did she say.
All were as if dead to her, or at least that's what she
pretended.

But I watch myself to keep past steps from becoming echoes,
to prevent what is gone from reverberating in a still
uncertain, impersonal and dubious present.
I am slightly uneasy at some level, not the one I now sense,
which is serene, but at the level where the soul encounters
invisible matter and confusion disperses.
The level where I admit to what's bothering me, to what has
hurt me, although not as I learned to say it, but silently and
in haste, like someone who fears being interrupted by death
and wants to take advantage of every second,
who fears hearing his own words and quickly hushes the
voices of his dream.

. . .

I surround myself with smoke, belching, the noise of bottles colliding and being uncorked, with drums and laughter, smooth faces and the passing glance of dresses.

Feeling how, at a certain distance from the days when we suffered, the mornings, afternoons and nights seem grimmer than they really were, more desolate as they vibrate in memory.

Full of eyes I can't see, of blindly groping hands.

Half the fat man explores, exposes warm places, like a king at the height of his pomp and ostentation.

Sitting on his lap, Persephone is a branch grafted on another trunk.

She is fondled from sun to moon, examined from thigh to thigh, and if the fat man should open his mouth, it's only to suck at her breasts. Breasts he can't grasp, because they're too big or because the clutching hands are too small.

The penumbra is gray, saturated with smoke. There's a real space for each body.

"We take off clothes, but we don't put them on," Susi says.

The obese man breathes noisily. He's inside and beside himself, as if he wanted to speak but couldn't. The music pours into his eyes, ears, nose. Persephone gives a fishy look.

Susi opens the hoop of her hands, and a man's semen drips from her fingers, like a brief, viscous, captive rainfall.

The onlookers applaud the musicians, who laugh back at them.

Some whistle, others shout.

The obese man whispers into my lady's ear, nibbles at her
breast. He lingers in the promised land. He rummages in her
sacred wood, her fountains and her temple.
He ogles her, squeezes a thigh, inspects her navel, guffaws.
A gelatinous white breast is crushed.

Drunkards abound, thickened dragging voices, belches like
unexpected commas drawing out a word, a sentence.
They hug each other to keep from falling, lean stupidly
against the columns. Heads bent, they maintain an innocuous
fury. Impudently observe what doesn't happen to them.
Sleep where lethargy encroached upon them.
They stumble, apologize to a shadow, to a shirt lying on the
floor next to a shoe.
They are singing loudly about how to deflower a virgin,
how to penetrate her, how to break into her and overcome
night and genital blood,
how she should respond with sobs of gratitude.
And afterwards her life will be easy and men necessary,
depending on the glory of her body, the glory of her loving.

Susi sings too, but more private lyrics in an undertone, just
for herself.
A lock of hair covers her left ear.
She's wearing a necklace.
Out of the darkness a hand grabs at one of her breasts,
another hand from the half-light murmurs to the other
breast.
But the song she is singing touches Susi more deeply.

Persephone sees the moon outside the window. A beam
traces a gray line on her face. Her hair hangs black and

springy over her bare back. There is nostalgia, savagery in
her expression.
She slides her clenched fingers down the pane, clawing at it.
She utters brief sentences which are more like groans than
words. She smiles, as if remembering a long-gone plot
against a long-gone being, or learning a person or object's
morbid secret.
The stain of penumbra on her neck is a mole.
She nervously twitches her foot, slowly withdraws it from the
shoe.
The obese man comes over to her, holds a small traveling
crucifix against her chest.
Persephone jerks away. Her face takes on an angry look.
Her back touches the wall. She walks off. Her thighs are
born. Her ankles are born. The floorboards quake beneath
her feet. She narrows her eyes, as if trying to keep an image
from escaping.
She leans against a column to the rear, unspeaking, her lips
quivering and swollen with rage.
Standing there next to the yellow plastic table, the
foot-tapping musicians, the pearly moon, there seems
to be an emptiness inside her where something was torn
from its place and needs time and rest to recompose
itself.
A strange quietude grips her. Her face becomes attentive, as
if listening to welcome news. Music, voices, noise can't
penetrate her self-absorption.
It is at such moments that the customers prefer her. Like
dogs, they sniff out the fear and solitude which can't stand
to be alone. They scent her discomfort, her uneasiness.
Quickly they gather round, waiting for the cry, the final
syllable of abandonment.

They congregate, silent and pale. Solemn with dissimulated
tension, they pretend to be respectable, converse.
They wait their turn, their summons, at her side.
Persephone looks at a streak on the wall.
She tears up the drawing she made, the random shapes she
hadn't even looked at.
Perhaps she's getting ready to work her way from one end to
the other, from bed to bed, from men she can't tell apart to
phalluses she subjugates with pleasure, as if she were breaking
a long fast not only of her own but of many hungers.

The masked women start to assemble.
The apparent leader is looking for her companions, who are
wrapped up in hairy arms. They join her one by one, like
petals reattaching themselves to a flower that isn't quite a
flower.
With the same walk and the same hint of annoyance they
cluster around the look that summons them.
Numerous customers tag after them, touching their thighs
and their breasts and telling dirty jokes which the masked
women don't understand.
The apparent leader is the first to disappear, to show the
way out.
The customers and their companions vanish in a throng
behind her, swept along by a will that is oblivious to them.

Persephone looks from a crumpled piece of paper to the
smoke floating like a cloud above her head to the obese
man's obscene white belly to her toes curling downwards.
The half-light comes at her from one direction and the hands
encircling her thighs from another.
She's completely on her own, in company.

. . .

The owner observes Susi's whiteness, Marta's pectoral guile,
Eva's swarthiness, what Susi's nose is smelling, the floozie's
eagerness, the flow of curtains and condoms, Magdalena's
soapy smell, mouths waiting for a chance to insult, bodies
and objects shifted from here to there.
He tracks the comings and goings of women who breathe
and crawl in the brothel, naked under their skirts, always
ready for combat with the blond or brunet musing at the
entrance.
He inspects the bathrooms, Norma's hips, a waiter's jacket,
Rosa's armpits, the musicians' euphoria, a customer's
joviality, both Marias' shadows;
the tables, corners, walls covered with eyes, columns covered
with words, laughter and fingerprints.
He slips a hand under Carmen's dress and investigates her
warm thighs.
He slips a hand inside a customer's shirt and tweaks his hair.
He kisses Norma on the neck and tickles her back.
He yanks down Maria's decolletage, cups a breast, shows it
to me.
He appraises a waiter's good evening, how he says, "Sit
down and make yourself at home."
He monitors the penumbra, a shadow on the wall, on the
chair, smoke beneath the ceiling, bodies embracing, what two
bald men are saying, the kisses Susi and a skinny man give
each other. He pokes Carmen in the belly, unties her ribbon,
musses her hair.
He checks on Carlota's bangs, her buttons, the shortness of
her skirt.
He measures the distance from Susi to Marta, from Susi to
Persephone, from Susi to me.

His pop-eyed stare brims over, starts walking, hangs among
the hats in the checkroom, asks for the bill in a sleepy
voice, goes outside with a customer, comes back in.

He enters copulation's dwelling, smiles at those who lie
there, touches their nudity, their arms, their sweat, winks at
them. Salutes the females who preside over these precincts,
offers them a young girl, the blood of a menstruating whore,
his own semen to use as they see fit.

He yawns in satisfaction, taps his finger on the unpainted
holes, pokes out a knot in the wood and through the opening
sees Carmen's knees.

When he scrutinizes, his expression freezes, his laughter
sticks in his throat, his eyes grow so big they almost burst.
His grandmotherly double chin droops.

He looks from one breast to another, from a sex to a cheek
to a waist. He spies with his whole body, his feet following
the walkers, his hands taking whatever other hands offer
him.

He witnesses with lips, eyebrows, gestures.

His eyes never rest, they promise novel attractions, cosseting,
virgins, downiness, fingernails, flat stomachs, overzealous
Persephones, copulation now and copulation later.

His entire being demands greater intensity, more nudity,
more amorous rhythms, more play of belly and hips, more
purposeful acts, more auguries of fornication.

He orders the women with good teeth to laugh, those with
pointy chins to throw their heads back, those with shapely
hands to show them off in studied ivory poses,

the blondes to flaunt their hair, those with beautiful eyes to
half-close them, to follow the most superfluous gesture,
those with unblemished knees to display them, the same for
those with voluptuous thighs, those with big breasts to thrust

them forwards, to clasp their hands behind their necks, and
the most attractive ones not to look at anyone, to walk
around delighting in themselves.
He's pleased by Marta, Rosamunda, Persephone's pleasures.
He fornicates when Carmen, Magdalena, Maria fornicate.
His hymen is broken along with the young girl's.
He throws wine in Carmen's eyes to shut her mouth.
He rouses Magdalena, who's dozing on her feet next to a
table, by slapping her behind as if it were her back.
He gives the floozie paper wings so she can fly, gives silver
coins to a waiter to make him smile.
Three gloomy women cheer up when they catch sight of him.
When he no longer looks at them, they become sad again.
Magdalena closes her purse at his signal.
At a signal, Carmen sways her hips to the music.
A woman who studies the floor as if following a trail stands
up when she feels his presence.
Mr. Moon and the lady of the full moons bow to him.
The musicians perk up as he goes by.
The very chairs and tables make way for him.
Emaciated women straighten up, suddenly slender and lithe.
He watches out of the corner of his unblinking fish eyes.
Sated by the food he hasn't eaten, he belches from lack of
appetite.
He is there beside the columns, he yawns in a corner,
coughs at the entrance, in the hallway.
Hurries two busboys clearing a table.
Shakes off Blanca's melancholy, says, "Don't you worry,
little momma."
Claps two customers who look like women on the back.
Infiltrates voices and gestures.
Scolds several whores. Questions a few young men about

their tastes, recommends Alma. Some of the customers laugh
when he interprets their dreams to attentive tarts.
He sleeps all day, keeps vigil all night.
Smiles constantly.
Notes how much wine and cigarettes are consumed.
Identifies the customers by which day of the week they visit
the brothel: this one is Monday, that one is Tuesday, the one
with the chin is Friday.
He peers under the table, measures the proximity of knees,
pushes them closer, separates them.
Eavesdrops on the men's propositions, the women's answers,
what they should say, what they should keep to themselves.
He hears if the musicians are in tune, if they're flagging.
He shatters inhibitions, bashfulness.
Prepares atmospheres and encounters.
His double chin sags suggestively.
Once he was a singer. He was born after seven months'
time.

Persephone laughs, as if her most private self came out in
laughter, as if an alien part of her erupted noisily into a life
of its own.
She rests her bare breasts on the obese man's shoulders,
drums her fingers on his head.
Her eyes are glistening, her cheeks pale. Hair partially hides
her face, and her forelock slides like a paintbrush across the
balding head.
Dressed in fondling and red light, her skin stands out in the
penumbra against the darker shades of the others, of the
bodies that graze her in passing.
She is sure of the water that will bathe her at dawn outside
the brothel, sure that nothing she does now will repeat itself,

since this moment will be debris in the next, a ruin she's too lazy to visit.

She scans each man, each object, content to drum on the obese man's head, on the small, gray, foreign world.

Her expression is suspended in another dimension, in an amazement so impersonal it could be the surprise felt by a woman over there when a finger delves between her thighs while she's talking.

She laughs. Lets each sound of laughter fall deliberately. Her gesture reaches out all of a sudden, now her hand is opening, now it rakes the man's neck, now leaves a trickle of blood, now it's over.

Her lips, which only reveal two white teeth, mutter words into the obese man's ear, words that thin out to turn into a cry of "Pig!" inside his head.

The man yawns, he's upset, he drinks the last drops from his glass, lets go of Persephone's thigh; he hides more than he's here, is here more than he's hidden.

He seems to lose contact with the floor, the chair, when he stands up, when he looks for a wall to lean against, and there is no wall.

A mockery hovers over his person. His perplexed humanness doesn't know what to think, what to do in this game that doesn't seem to be a game.

His little eyes look into the others' faces as if he were searching for a mirror to see himself, to learn what features he'd acquired recently.

Not only do the customers appear to know him, but they see too much of him, they penetrate that creature he doesn't believe is himself, whose body is visible in fits and starts, in the mute complaints sweating through each pore of his skin.

He slashes the smoke, the penumbra, with sudden
movements. Makes noise with words. His hand threatens, his
finger warns, he gropes towards the darkness: doesn't find
her.
His anger becomes audible. His plump hand comes and goes.
The shortness of his arm stretches out and contracts. Caught
in the act, he looks at me. Doesn't move. Watches me. Just
for a moment.
His face is red, blue, black, depending on the space he's
crossing.
Persephone is right behind him. If he turns around, if he
moves, she's behind him. She tickles and pokes his behind,
spits on his head, claws at the skin hanging in quivering
folds on his neck. Her nails leave behind four arcs of blood,
furrows, paths. Wakes of raw flesh are drawn, intersect,
overlap, branch out.
He spins around. Raises his left foot, then his right foot.
Heaviness oozes out of his flanks. He slaps at the darkness,
throws slow punches quickly into the void.
He huffs. Snorts. Sweats through his unbuttoned shirt,
outraged innocence burning in his cheeks and ears. A look
of utter repugnance has come over his face.
Persephone says, as she pulls his hair, that she's covering
him with lice.
Persephone says that she's throwing flies at his hands.
She shoves against his paunch a drunken, bovine slut, who
doesn't breathe a single word or complaint as she crashes
into him.
She hurls hard ice cubes at his face, his chest.
She blindfolds him with a wet napkin, on which she
sprinkles a few drops of wine.

Fatso takes out his wallet and shows her his most precious
bill.
"It's like my son," he explains.
"Take it and leave me alone. I never want to see you
again."
"You'll never see it again," Persephone answers, and tears it
up.

The man is leaving at last.
But she holds him back. Slips a noose of arms around his
neck. Pummels his chest.
One on top of the other, they reach the exit. He tries to
shake her off. Four bald men jeer at him. A woman, a fiction
in dress and glasses, laughs. She's pregnant, about to give
birth, but still she laughs.

The obese man puts his hand in his mouth.
Persephone licks the nape of his neck and his ears. Calls
him by my name. Gently kicks him.
Opaque, greasy stares follow them in their impalement.
He sweats out of dismay, more exhausted at each step. He
tries to say something which recedes farther inside him
instead of gushing out.
Harried, he looks at my face and the other faces looking at
him.
Persephone hangs on him. Spells words on his back, blows
the letters of my name on his neck.
Tries out different ways of calling him by other names.
But he doesn't hear. He shuffles his swollen feet impatiently.
His eyes command the others to help him, to forgive him.
He crouches before us beseechingly.

Takes three stealthy rapid steps which are not enough to
free himself.
Is still burdened, held captive. He inflates and deflates his
cheeks.
The customers no longer join in or sneer. They stare at him
as if drawn to an irresistible object.

Persephone and the obese man grapple, pushing against the
curtain with their bodies, a movement away from rolling
down the stairs.
Both are flushed in the reddish light. The shading of their
faces alters as he changes his tactics.
Two customers try to separate them, although their method
consists in grabbing at Persephone's breasts, one apiece.
The owner hurries over. He chides Persephone. Holds her
arms. Pulls her hair. Loudly reproaches her bad behavior.
Pushes her and the fat man against the wall. Sticks an unlit
cigarette in her mouth.
While she recovers the fat man walks out furiously.
So that the pent-up collective laughter will spatter over
Persephone and the owner standing at the entrance.
So that the hour can come in through the window as a
witness, as one more inquisitive, throbbing sound.
Almost at dawn.

Out of all the musicians, only one sings intelligibly.
He scarcely moves as he sings, wan and trembling.
A customer comes from one end of the room, a customer
comes from the other end. They meet up near me, hug each
other, ask "How are you?" and "What have you been
doing?" They sit down at a table. The old whore's kids
appear. They're kids because they've never grown up.

They're the brothel's dwarves. The labels read: Armando,
Alfredo.
Smoke trickles from Maria's mouth.
Magdalena is upset by what the owner tells her. Resting her
chin on her right hand, Marta becomes pensive.
Maricarmen smiles.
Smooth hand insinuates itself into Cristina without even
grazing her thighs.
The owner cleans his pipe.

Persephone moves from table to table. Leaves ashes and a
cigarette butt at one. Examines the checkered tablecloth. The
vase.
She sighs, full of worries. Speaks in measured tones to a
man. Turns her head towards me.
She sits down.
Stretches out her feet and wiggles them. Folds and unfolds
her hands. Her pout ignores memories, ignores those
present.
Her body is still. She stares blankly at the palm of her left
hand. She listens without hearing, looks without seeing.
Suddenly she brightens up, seems to be all movement. Blows
on the water in a glass. Spills a few drops when she does it
again.
Opens her handbag. Takes out a compact. Crosses her legs.
Flips open the compact. Sticks out her chin. Fluffs her hair.
Breathes out as if ridding herself of a weight on her chest.
She powders her face. Scatters fine powder. Puts lipstick on.
Shuts the compact.
The handbag is still open.
She looks at her palm again, with the nail of her right pinky
traces its lines, its labyrinth of omens and doubts.

Follows a long line to its end. Nonchalantly starts on
another. Is frightened by its brevity.
Drops her hand.
Smoke dissolves against the black ceiling.
Everywhere there are cigarettes, knees and penumbra.

Susi sings along with the musicians. Opens her black coat.
Underneath she has no blouse on, no brassiere, no skirt—
only bare skin, only an epidermic dress of shapes, only a
triangular medallion.
Maria is arguing. She lowers her voice abruptly, like
someone who can't find the right words, or who feels the
words retreating, shriveling on her tongue.
A customer's eyes flicker, pierced by advertisements, by
spot-lit objects seen at random, by clocks telling the time.
There's an empty cigarette box on the nearest table, and a
lily her admirers gave the floozie for her birthday.

Persephone stands up. She's coming towards me, but
apparently too slowly.
For a moment she seems distant, arrested.
With the tranquility of someone who wakes in the middle of
a dream and knows she will fall asleep again, and soon does,
she sits down once more.
The floozie takes a dirty spoon, a knife, a fork, a plastic
glass, an orange, a napkin out of a bag.
Pours water from a bottle. Slices a lemon. Spoons sugar into
the glass. Stirs the contents.
Dumps some canned macaroni and fried meat on a plate.
Bites off a piece of bread, a piece of meat.
She looks at the floor while she eats, drinks, and regresses
into long-lost domestic habits.

A man says hello, stops to chat, seems impatient, in a hurry, telling her something between titters and yawns. Soon after he moves on.

Once again she is left alone. A match lights up her face. She holds a green doll on her lap, pretending to speak to it, to pamper it.

She props her elbows on the table. Combs her eyebrows with a toothbrush.

Puts the bread into the bag. The spoon. The fork.

Lights up a cigarette. Savors each puff. Looks at a customer. Winks, waggles her fingers.

The customer comes nearer, examines her from six feet away, and speaks. She uncovers a breast.

He reveals a toothless mouth. Drooling on his chest he sits down next to her, talks to her in a nervous shrill voice.

He places the lily from the other table between her hands.

Dawn is gathering. The noon of night has gone. The first gleams of daylight disclose its temperature.

Stone takes on color. Treetops are roots of the day yet to grow.

The moon, silver necklace from which Venus dangles like a pearl, still sheds its brightness.

The abyss is only perspective, location.

There will be nests on some branches.

Persephone offers me a glass of wine, which I refuse. She shrugs her shoulders. Dashes the wine in my face, it slides down my neck, wets my back. My eyes are burning.

Susi and the owner snigger, very close to each other. The music expands, increasingly hoarse and out of tune. I wipe off my lips, ears and chin with my handkerchief, dry my hair.

The furtive witnesses believe I'm paying tribute for an
offense against her. They couldn't care less.
No causality is possible for those yellow socks, only acts. For
those wide blue jackets, those narrow foreheads, there is no
remembering, no thought, no justification.
The music and dancing continue despite the smarting eyes,
the unexpectedness and the excuses.
Susi's words are more real than the night. When dealing
with the indispensable prostitute you must kneel, you must
exhale politely, you must be masculine and lavish.
All reflection is suspect in the reddish penumbra, in the
jubilant crowd.
The only straight path climbs to Maria's nipples, descends
from Maria's breasts.
Time belongs to the drunks dancing clumsily, their arms
linked together.
All the rest doesn't count, it's boring. Other behavior
scarcely matters, is almost scandalous.
Hearts and genitals mesh gears, add up their years, relish
each other.
They aim at a spot they call reality and hit the target,
denying their surroundings, the past, the present.

Persephone recites a few verses in French which she had
told me in secret. Acting them out she touches her thighs,
her stomach, her hips.
In front of everyone she emphasizes practices that are not
mine, that she's learned from others and, while performing
them, mistakes for mine.
She points her finger at me, half-closing one eye as if aiming
at a quarry that has already been caught and digested, but is

hungered for all over again, desired anew when it is seen to
be alive once more.
She opens up to them as she did to me. Holds out her hand
just as I hold out mine. Strokes herself just as I stroke her.
Inhabits the possessed, the possessor.
She pours out secrets over those who watch and will repeat
them, obsessions, intimacies, reproaches against me.
She lays bare nakedness hidden within walls.
She delights in being seen, in sharing with others the
intertwined solitude, the moment when two forces meet,
annihilate and cancel each other out.
I am seeing how I enter her body as if entering a grave, how
I emerge from it as if resurrected, how I lie there afterwards,
trembling and slow of thought.
She divulges the sceptical gesture with which she receives
me, the way I move into her warm zones, the trouble she
has expelling me, pushing me aside.
She makes public my expression, my husky voice, the
moment which is and isn't mine.
I see myself ensnared, overwrought, embedded in her loins,
in her difficult rhythm of pursuit and endurance.
Customers and whores are watching, they seize on and
discard what has remained of me in her, as well as what
hasn't remained.
And I feel we have never been alone, that faces have been
spying on our solitude, hands that are neither hers nor mine
have been fondling her;
that there has been more eagerness, more panting, more
savage fingernails, more lacerating energy on her body from
the others, than in my caresses insinuated between doubt
and desire;

that this music and these faces are more commonplace, more
visible, more present, that they live inside her with greater
force than I do;
that this groundswell of laughter and these eyes which
despair of using her reach a depth I have never plumbed.

The night air is less hostile. A few stars come in through the
window, go out through the window. The street light settles
like fog.
Outside nobody's dogs chase indistinct stragglers, sniff at
them, assimilate their smells and keep following them.
Distant noises are heard, voices seeking no one in deserted
alleyways.
A hooker passing by the window looks in, spits in front of
her feet and goes on her way as if a ghost were pushing her.
She doesn't look back. Her dress flutters in an invisible
wind. The clattering of her shoes is all the silence that
surrounds her.
Beings, or perhaps shadows, go by, heads bent, eyes glued to
the ground, driveling about ridicule, wasted hours,
what-you'd-like-to-be. They are pallid, night is in their hands
and their faces in the night, as if each one carried the
brothel inside him and even without having to go in,
responded to it with the last string of his aspirations.
They walk on. It doesn't matter on which night or in which
season of the year. Feeling the same chill. Staring at the icy
flagstones, the gray pavement.
In harmony with the kingdom. Where a knife is blood, and
blood a flow that slowly silences a shout.
Where rage is God the Father, and all else is unbelievable.
Where the trap is set, instantaneous and perpetual.
Because, it is said, that once the tree of the twelve fruits

grew here, and because, it is said, that there's a spot where you can see a pillar of light.

Magdalena strips from the waist down. Smiles at her spectators.
Susi goes out on the dance floor, spreads her legs apart like someone recalling a lewd position who makes her recollection visible.
The floozie throws away a burning piece of paper, like a misshapen bird, like a flaming lance.
Blanca explains that her bones ache, that bread makes her nauseous.
A customer touches some breasts, which are Persephone's.
The thighs he touches now are her thighs.

There's a young girl with meager breasts whose laugh could unsettle the whole creation.
There's a big-eyed man who blushes when touched, and who responds to pursuit with platitudes.
There's a boy who's in the habit of adopting feminine poses. His hair hangs down to his backside. His face is as sore as a nursing nipple. They call him Eugenia, or Elizabeth III.
There are four professional ladies, who don't know what to do with their hands. Scrawny and heavily powdered, they look in the same direction, greet the same person, speak in the plural, as if they had mislaid "I did it, it was I."
There's a blot which suddenly becomes color, sound, waiter.
There's a swarthy girl impressionable youths rub against for inspiration.
There's a fetal night in many eyes, an old man painted at a picture's edge who sleeps suspended in the air on seagull wings.

There's a gray-haired fellow in a red shirt who wants to
redeem Carmen, and who is in her way wherever she turns,
too effusive not to be suspect.
There is murmuring and music and the sound of breaking
glasses. Tables and chairs in clusters and shadowy corners.
There's fire and noise in the bodies making love. There's a
flame inside us that feels nostalgia for the sun, and winter
nesting in us as a transient guest. There are prostitutes
trampled by too numerous admiration.

Here's that weakling, more real than my thought which
denies him.
Here's the other one, who prefers young girls and old ladies,
because they're not yet or already have been women.
Here's the Hodgepodge, an old crone so called because her
explanations never explain what she means.
Here's a whore who fondles a customer's knees as if she
were fondling the heads of the twins quickening in her belly.
Here's a woman whose leg, hand, eye and ear were cut away
on the operating table, a grievous loss, although she
confesses they were of no use to her.
Here's Persephone. Here's Susi, who points to Marta, Jazmín
and Rosamunda and says to me, "We're on your side, but
you don't pay attention to us."
Here's a happiness which can only be entered headfirst, by
way of a sex, a breast, a mouth, an ear or sheer confusion.
Here is what isn't here, more present than what, because of
its visibility, makes us doubt our very existence.
Here are people whose lack of satisfaction increases with
their satiety;
sluts who can't furnish even one second of genuine oblivion,

who ramble over the heart's surface and are the same as
when they first came here, despite the years gone by and the
worm gnawing at their insides;
beings who only know the shadow attached to their feet;
those who understand less about life than they imply, more
than they admit to;
the young tarts who are a whole river of perfumes in one
body;
the women whose faces record the ebb and flow of the tides,
the moon's punctuality;
the women who dream of souls which in one night have
flown straight to the stars.

The owner nods his head, unbuttons his jacket, lowers his
hands. He stops the music.
The musicians lay down their instruments, group behind
him, wait for his next move.
The echo of the song they were playing still lingers in the
feet of two couples.
The waiters are deaf to anyone who calls them as they clear
away glasses, plates and plastic forks.
Rosa, Alma, Carla emerge from copulation's dwelling; they
jingle the keys, look at Carmen's back.
Cooks and dishwashers surface among the customers, chat
with them, converse with the women; once out of uniform
they blend into the citizenry.
Chairs, tables, corners, bathrooms are vacated, and slowly
appear as what they are.
Several customers hunt for cigarette butts in the ashtrays,
others argue with the busboys over a broken glass. Quite a
few sprawl across the tables like unclaimed packages.

The owner rouses the sleepers roughly, pulling their hair and
shoving them.
The floozie dances with outstretched arms, without music.

White profile looks at me sideways. Almost invisible black
braids hang from the woman's face turning towards me, like
a female St. John the Baptist placing her disembodied head
on a platter of shadows.
The little bells signal closing time.
The lights go on and off twice.
The twelve columns in the big room gleam momentarily.
Twelve bodies leaning against them also gleam. Tables,
yawns, stockings, hands which want to go on exploring
gleam.
Customers and whores wake up.
Eyes, feet, trousers, hips start moving.
Mute and expectant, the instruments remain on the stage.

Dawn enters like a silent reveille, darkness retreats,
crumbles.
Colors begin to scatter in subversive specks.
The customers' voices shuttle back and forth, making hasty,
desperate plans.
Shouting "bitch" and "whore" the owner shakes Susi
against the wall; his attitude is "this isn't me, it's someone
else, it's her soul that's hitting her."
Bells and lights announce closing time.
You can see hundreds of eyes opening with difficulty; you
know there are many more than you had thought in the
penumbra.
A throng of people stirs, stretches, flows out into the street.
There's an exodus of mouths, legs, noses, breasts and hair.

There's a bustle in the hallway, in the checkroom, at the tables, at the entrance.

Margarita and Maria, Carmen and Rosamunda, Blanca and Cristina mingle with the others on their way out.

I overhear a man with rubber lapels complaining angrily to another man about the disadvantages of the brothel's closing so early.

I see how the owner's eyes become inquisitorial.

I hear a man and a woman haggling over her price and the cost of a hotel room.

The noise the prostitutes, waiters, customers and busboys make going out.

I hear how the night leaves behind an animality, a spoor.

I see that some leave easily, others tumble down the stairs, falling outside into the dawn with all their might, or seem helpless and dizzy, as if they had just been ejected from their mothers' wombs, or don't want to leave at all, and stand mute and stolid turning their inebriation into deafness and misunderstanding, or lie stretched out on the floor like dead men in their coffins, wanting to prolong night in the depths of their own night, or will no longer descend the steps since they fell down already without noticing how far they could fall.

Persephone takes my arm.

Her way of walking is slow, weary. She looks at her feet, at the floor.

Her mouth seems larger, her eyes smaller, her nose sharper and redder.

She doesn't notice the customers saying goodbye to her, doesn't feel the owner patting her back.

She goes down step by step, almost tenderly, as night and
daybreak struggle in her face.
She looks older; a trace of melancholy puckers her lips.
Her coat falls off, she picks it up.
Something I hadn't remarked in her hand turns out to be a
flower.

Going backwards is also downwards, now is also upwards.
There's a sound of breaking ribs as drunkards topple over.
Eye by eye, tooth by tooth, wound by wound, they climbed
up, they came down.
They were born in time and in places.
They keep coming out, like newborn babies into the dust.
They emerge groping like blind men (or grotesque idols) and
go off as one.
They emerge under such an intense light that their bodies
seem overexposed.
The colors of their suits look faded, worn away, old.
Soon they begin to leave, vanish down alleys, shapes
rendered unreal by dawn.

Whores sashay out the door. The waiter who slaps people on
the back exits.
Maria yawns at the threshold.
The floozie departs with a young man. Rosa and Rosario
together.
Persephone glitters alone, a light torn from the darkness.
Just one instant outside suffices to free her from the night's
embroideries.
Her hands are shaking.

· · ·

The owner stays inside the brothel, which finally closes.
The heavy doors groan and creak.
They also groan inside me.

Under the tranquil sky the brothel has the look of a haven
of forgetting and repose.
Susi is a shadow escaping from the light. She turns a corner.
Droopy-eyed drunks piss in the gutter.
Dogs bark at them and they wander off.

That woman over there is a red blot. That man staring at
her goes towards her.
She guides his head inside her dress. Shows him tangible,
fragrant darkness.
He touches her thighs beneath the dress.
(His hands become eyes.)
The fish feels the baited hook forming a concavity, a
compelling curve inside him.
"One of these breasts," she says, "is called Trial, and the
other is Tribulation, and when I squeeze them—like this—
milk comes out."

And I shake Persephone off me. I withdraw my head from the
darkness of her dress, from the tangible fragrance of her thighs.
And I wake up like the man who usually sleeps with the
light on to keep away the ghosts and having once turned it
off by mistake, feels he is someone else and wakes up
elsewhere, and in order to become himself again must
identify the furniture, his own lethargy, the languor that has
possessed him.
And I rise and walk as if I knew the way, but don't want to
take it.

Persephone, look at that man going outside backwards; he dreams inside out and we have to turn him upside down to see his real face.

Look at the others, fugitives from the fetus, men who have no glory, no fetishes, no vindication. Melancholy erupts in them like a bad habit.

Look at them once and for all, and if you want to save yourself from Medusa, try not to turn your head in their direction. Otherwise the blind time of their absence will fall upon your time.

It will fall. But you dare.

You soar vibrantly above this blatant dawn.

Some profound galactic memory disturbs the very center where your longings hover, and your mad desire to flee transfigured through the air dissolves.

A chance stammering hidden by dust, by flame, may grow within you, destroy you, say ancient words to you that once were powerful.

But you persevere, you speak now and you will speak tomorrow.

It's impossible to get inside you, to share your life. You prolong yourself.

Each span of earth is a landing place. Each instance marks your passage.

You speak of dreams that only project reality, you speak of realities that are dreams.

Laughter, foreign languages and sighs come from the same direction, from the same street corner, at times from the same shadow.
Faces and lost objects make surprise attacks, call out from where they lie in disuse.
The bell tolls over sparkling new minutes, and your body contracts at the hazy edge of sound.

She is walking, a mute radiance in the morning.
She sheds bodies on the gray pavement, in the ashen time that is burning up.
She turns toward me eyes fixed upon her own gaze.
Then she laughs.
Then she walks on.
Night retreats like a muffled lover, whom the brightening air pushes towards the dark.
The shades become a white wall, a peaceful river.

The black time turns green.
No color is immobile, no sound is silent.
The first blue will be the day's blue.

Creation awakens.
Day exists as on the first day.
Darkness cleaves from light, the heights from the depths.
Dawn already touches the hills, the cathedral dome, pierces

the eyelids of what still sleeps (without dreaming) and a
bird's eyes.
The sun restores to each thing its own movement, its image
between heaven and earth. It irradiates this immense
dwelling like a great candle bathing a child's hand in light.
The world is born in a flame.

Everything is a thought, barely a dream.
Dawn and whiteness of invisible feathers.
Voices hush, noises start up.
Things have surface, edges.

All space vibrates with light.
Roofs, trees, song are visible.
Silence overflows its sounds.
The bottom appears.
Everything is alive.

Yellow lives.
Violet opens its eyes and looks.
Red bursts forth in an epiphany.
The universe of the stars is the universe of the eye.
All that light grazes reverberates.
Dawn, noon, twilight, night, motley afternoon are all
reflected in a moving cloud.
Everything that glitters is an eye of images.

A piece of paper flies toward you.
It says your name.
An ever-ascending splendor falls towards you.
It says your name.
A young day envelops you.

It says your name.
A flood of sun releases real birds and birds of light.
It says your name.
A shadow no longer a shadow, beheld by the sun.
It says your name.
Something blue winging beneath the blueness.
It says your name.
Something that falls like a flame on your arms.
It says your name.
Something that rises from your heart.
It says your name.

Light reigns.
The just light.
The virgin light.

With a love equal to the first love, it swaddles each creature
with its body.
Always preceding the word.
Always the most certain of appearances, of transparencies.
Everything it touches is sacred.
Everything it looks at shines.

The just light.
Finds a nest in the place it chooses, like a bird.
Steps with winged foot on the stone's repose, the sap of
plants, the woman's eyes, the thousand shapes of the beast.

Persephone advances pressing against me. What is hers is
excessive, what belongs to her. What is mine is trifling, this
oppression, the impossibility of walking like this.

We go along a street that descends. We go down it arm in
arm and descending. The upward slant follows us closely.
We give off smoke and ashes. We look at this sloping
fragment of world.
The street stretches ahead, luminous and empty. A dog that
was run over stares at us, its intestines quivering, its eyes
glassy, its paws stiffened. Daybreak flutters everywhere, like
an apparition we become used to easily and without fear.

We are a seed, a breath, a shadow. The height makes us
giddy. The ground picks us up and raises us.
We are more than one hundred faces growing in our faces,
more than one hundred names nesting in our names.
We see each other as if through an unsilvered mirror.
I am not dreaming or sleeping or keeping watch. Health
inhabits me. King of my kingdom.
Persephone is weightless. She floats on a moving current.
Her face, her smile are golden-green.
We keep on walking. Impelled by something, but not
somebody.
The earth is a dawn. Fire, air and water cradle us.
We reach a square.

Silence curls Persephone's lips. She half-closes her hands.
Smiles.
And like someone who's thinking of pleasant things, and
who, upon realizing she's smiling to herself, forgets what she
was thinking about, she stops smiling.
And then smiles again, as if she had a vision and afterwards
the visitation of what she saw in the vision: she feels doubly
enlightened.
Not expecting from the instant any moment other than the

instant itself. Not expecting any face other than her own face.
Her eyes are wide-open and wary, as if she were listening to light clearing a path in her body, among the leaves.

An ashtray falls from a second-story window, breaks into ten clay fragments.
People are burning incense in a room, they perfume their shadows and turn their dread into a ritual.
A bare-shouldered girl leans out of a window combing her hair.
Her bright eves open to a youthful brightness.

The metal shutters, the mouths, the genitals, the windows have fallen behind. Absence has also fallen, clenching into a fist—a brothel—shut up in itself.
The whores have gone and everything that reminds us of them.
Those who are imprisoned beyond the borders of life, outside their bodies, have gone.
Death didn't come from here or there. It was inside us, our guest, it had our face, the gestures of our hands.
It dreamed of chairs, words, dreamers.

No one else in this dawn will pursue the red body, the masks' grimace, a blond's pale rebuff.
The mirror's reflection of a fool's leer will no longer be required.
Never again shall we see the eyes we saw there.

Even if they return tonight and look at us, with one day more in their black pupils, one step closer to the habit they are concealing, with one more moonlight in their immodesty.

Even if tonight, when they get up, they turn each hour into a time for impurity, into a stepping-stone to imperceptibly reach their own cadaver.

No one else in this dawn will chase after Persephone, will bury his future death in her entrails.
The customers will move in real space, in the terror, the chasm that separates one body from another.
For a whole day the brothel will be an eye fallen from the face of the sky.
It will be stone and brick, venetian blinds and windows.

We climb towards memory and death down the sloping street and around the corner, passing whitewashed houses and green walls, with every step and every movement, in each inward and outward look.
And our name is a whisper, a nothing once it's pronounced, and we ourselves like those who have to look back from time to time to see if someone who was once theirs is still following, or is about to lag behind, or get lost.
And the pillar of salt is more an omen than a reminder.

We will climb up to the dim evening, to the gathered shadows, to the yawn gaping in a mouth of mildew and decay.

We will take faces, tables, freedom and poison against suffering.
While a voice over a microphone that defiles what is said announces music for love.

.   .   .

Gradually the brothel will fill up with adolescents and
middle-aged women, with the curious and the self-confident,
with incessant smoke and lethargic seconds.
The noise and the songs will drown out words, muffle sobs.
Persephone will take the sixth table, the one with flowers
and four ashtrays.
And when she dances, you can almost believe that the man
is embracing what was inapprehensible even for her, a
celestial patrimony, like the soul.

But that won't be surprising, just one more misfortune she'll
have to repudiate, with my help.
For I will be at her side, trying to extricate her from her
troubles, from her convictions.
So that her mouth, which has lost some of its primal
amazement, can secretly exorcise itself.

Persephone walks inside her body, outside her body. She
looks away.
She picks a flower in passing, plucks off one flaming petal.
She throws her head back. Looks at the sky, at the petal.
Walks on.

A waiter comes towards us along the opposite sidewalk: he's
free when the brothel is closed, when the owner goes to
sleep in the arms of some cheap whore.
He inhabits baggy striped trousers, inflated by a chill wind.
He looks at his feet without finding anyone. His hands in his
pockets are not waiting for the Messiah.
He disappears around a corner as silently as he came.

. . .

A monkey caged in glass scratches its armpit and makes
faces, on display in a storefront.
A heap of dark clouds agglomerates in the distance.
Persephone looks at the tall unlit windows, at the lamps still
on in the streets, yellowish and pale.
Vapor comes out of her mouth. Sleep is on her eyelids.
The wind has a girl's laugh, a swift bodiless summons which
finds its form raising dust.
The morning settles in slowly, touches walls, buildings,
ground.
We are gods walking with the sun in our faces.

We reach a park. The tiled pavement is blue. The benches
are vacant, gray. A crumpled newspaper seems shriveled by
solitude.
A boy riding a bicycle comes and goes.
Persephone sneezes. Then she speaks to me: she's cold.

A tree grows upwards and downwards; among its branches is
the root that rises like a light among the leaves.
Facing all directions, full of itself, full of birds that are a
whole generation of birds, it continuously flickers their eyes,
their countless wings.

We continue walking.
We turn the corner.
We see a house which has sharp angles, a white facade and
tall windows.
A man is talking to himself. Behind him a shadow is
listening.
A moth gone astray in the daylight nestles into itself to keep
from being dazzled. And

. . .

the song of the silent dawn is too intense for me
Persephone's light steps are too quick for me
this luminosity is too similar
to the shape of my eyes
not to feel that something of mine
glistens in the dawn and in her.

The key grinds, almost breaking in the lock.
I have trouble pushing the door open. I hold it ajar while
she goes in.
And we go inside, feeling like those who saw all the light
disappear at once, before stepping over the threshold of a
dark cave.
The courtyard leading to the staircase turns out to be
deserted and gloomy.
A light bulb at the edge of the roof is turned on but doesn't
give light.
The staircase has a few steps that are broken or too close
together, but at least we can climb up without risk of falling
to the bottom.

We go up hand in hand, two steps at a time.
First one floor.
Then another.
Finally the last one.
We go up.
I climb the stairs thinking: first flight, three steps.
I see this window. I see another window.
I climb and I remember that I'm walking over other
footsteps, that I am what I was, that I live now what I have
never been.

The small door to the room opens noiselessly.
The yellow light opens up familiarly.
The furniture, in their places, seem naked, the alien
furnishings of dreams.
We hear the shrill voices of vigilant old women, unruly
children who are nothing but sobs.
Hoarse curses come through the wall.
Persephone takes off her coat, shoes, stockings, dress.
Undoes her hair, sits down on an armchair. Yawns as if
ridding herself of who knows what.
A king of spades molders at the bottom of a wastepaper
basket.
"What I'm thinking," she says, "is scary."

There are glasses, playing cards, ashtrays, knives, a stuffed
bird, a hand which is mine on the table.
Pale-colored curtains cover the windows.
She and I sit still and silent, separated under the dawn
erupting drowsily outside.

I look at them and I look at myself; exhausted by something
that doesn't even take your breath away, entrenched in the
irreparable, living blindly in a hopeless situation, frivolous in
pain and frivolity.
Floating on a planet that itself is in motion, passing through
a time that also runs out, dying of a death which dissociates
plants and animals alike, twilights and stars, memories and
words, spurious acts and genuine movements.

Dawn quiets a cat's mewings.
I draw the curtains. The hanging clothes sway slowly. Lower
down, in the street, three people are moving about.

I close the curtains. I smoke. Persephone says to me:
"If I eat this cookie, the cookie turns into me."
Surfeited even before eating, she eats it.
Turned into me, because I loved her, a woman inhabits me,
and I am that woman, and I am myself, and she is the man
who I am, and she is herself.
In search of her manner I am her manner.
But not entirely.
I look at them and I look at myself. I feel I am going away,
that I am not them. I feel that I am breathing and myself
again, someone who had left and suddenly returns.

Persephone opens the cupboard. Takes out a bottle. A smell
of cloves, of spices wafts by.
She pours water from one container to another.
She stretches her arms, says to me:
"There are people who like to make their lives insignificant;
I don't want to go by unnoticed."

The fat woman breathed deeply, like an athlete getting ready
for a long race with no time out. She patted her hair. Shut
her purse. With a smile decided to begin.
But first she squeezed Persephone's hand, looked in our
eyes, yanked her skirt down, peevishly cast a look about her
to see if anyone was spying on us.
She said:
"There's a trip in your lives, a disastrous separation, a
spiritual, psychological, physical upheaval. In short, a dry
death from head to foot.
You will not reach the last gasp together, you will not share
the years which precede the consummation of your earthly
life.

You will journey alone, vulnerable, mistaken and barren.
A prejudice, a misunderstanding, a rigidity, a differing
mental velocity, some kind of promiscuity, will cause you to
break up.
Neither will be prepared to repair the damage.

You will both sleep in unrepentant waters with bodies that
don't belong to you, that neither add nor take away
anything, but do make you waste time.
Sleeping in each other's arms, making love, eating together,
going out, agreeing when you could easily disagree, can give
you the illusion of permanence.
Only the illusion.
The immediacy of love usually dazzles us and we want to
hold it fast. But love, like light and thought, is a long-term
force we're still not able to tolerate.
As for the doubts which others' failures cause in us, we seek
the exception, we want to be realities in the passing mirage,
alter its contours and what we are.
We shoot our arrows at a vague date, and our poor darts
don't even reach the next minute, they disappear as soon as
they're shot, leaving traces of something that fluttered.
What we weave in solitude is unraveled by the doorbell's
ringing, by the wind rattling an open window, by a man and
a woman who aren't part of the plot and who watch us with
burdensome curiosity.
The scornful words of a third person, whom we never
suspected, can decide the outcome, snatch away the tightrope
when we're trying to keep our balance.
Everything is contingent. Everything participates.
One man's belch jars us from the right mood to place us in
his belching, the hand of a beggar in the street makes us

give without giving, see without seeing. One night she will
go away, for one of the already mentioned reasons, but she
won't know exactly why. Driven by a hazy but certain,
uncertain desire.

We open boxes that concern us and that don't concern us,
that take us elsewhere and leave us in the same place,
perplexed in a fragment of perplexity.

We emerge from one tunnel only to enter another. We open
one box only to find another inside.

Everything is silent, everything cries out.

Between one body and another there's an abyss, there's
union.

She will go away, fleeing almost anxiously, but without really
knowing where she's running from; without really going
away, because relinquishing is not going away.

And even though you share her life minute after minute, you
won't be able to share it completely, even though you do
share it at times.

And the book you will write about your loss will not recover
any of her affection in the future. It will be nothing more
than a trace describing another trace.

That will be thirty-seven pesos and fifty cents.

Everything I've said can be verified. Thank you very much.
Come back soon. Perhaps the auguries will change.

Excuse me. But there are others waiting.

I can hear their yawns from here, their complaints, their
eagerness to know what's ahead, what happened so
enigmatically it's as if it hadn't happened yet, as if I could
tell them it's a portent.

Just to reassure them. A crutch for the cripple, false hands
for the maimed, golden marbles for the blind, a smile for the
fool and for me sleep without dreams at the bottom of sleep.

And goodbye again.
And again I ask you to come back soon, not to forget me.
And perhaps.
And perhaps, if you consult me once more, you'll never
break up, and I'll tell you good omens."

I laughed wildly, wavering between laughter and trembling.
Persephone gently smoothed her hair, as if confirming that it
was still in the same place. Then she looked with boredom
at the fortune-teller.
The fat woman said: "Don't provoke the spirits. Believe, if
you wish . . . that laugh, those gestures, that boredom were
foreseen."

And perhaps, if I hadn't known what is forbidden, there
wouldn't be this insolation over things, a very nocturnal
insolation, with its respective black suns.
My days would not be stange moments, a strange flight,
gusts of smoke, stammerings that fall unresisting into a
limbo I want to make solid, just to hide myself in it.
Persephone's hands wouldn't be cause for upset, disquieting
softness, signs of a life that perseveres and continues beyond
my comprehension.
Nostalgia wouldn't bring back gifts from the past, village
lights watching me fleetingly from a train.
I wouldn't fidget nervously when everything around me is
calm, projects quietude. I wouldn't fail to recognize familiar
beings when I open my eyes, disconsolate in the middle of
the night.
This need to force things, to avail myself of what has always
been denied to others, while buoying me up also destroys
me.

The agile movement, the coldness of nudity live inside me.
Rapid icy words transfix men and objects with spite and
fancy.
And it's possible that the brothel dwellers, the spineless
sluts, the men for hire by the first comer, measure the
strength of my intentions, despise the worthlessness of my
achievements.
I've had more desires than chances, than right moves. I've
seen the craving to burn with one's own flame consume itself
in ambition.
I slip and fall on superfluous doubts, in a schedule that
could be managed easily, because the solution is obvious.
And facing the danger that I am inventing for myself I note
certain absences, certain forces that have deserted me,
certain snapshots of myself here and there:
remembering what I have and haven't been, what I still am
not, what I will never be.
And I see how the moments of pleasure belong to the
ineffable, and what I have salvaged survives in the invisible,
and any absolution, any exegesis is in vain.
And I suspect that the poets' silence is not accidental, but
only one more string plucked in secret by the wind.

On the windowpanes day taking hold dissolves reflections, an
insect buzzes caught in the trap.
The clock's hands advance noiselessly. The chair, the
bed, the books, the chess set, the photographs remain in
place.
Persephone eats a piece of bread while she shakes a white
tablecloth out the open window.
She throws a broom on the floor, like a reaper getting rid of
the sickle that wearies him. Moves a small trunk, a scarf, an

umbrella cover. She opens a drawer, opens up a musty,
odorous intimacy.

She finishes undressing, as if obeying a desire less
instinctive than cerebral.

She looks at herself furtively in the mirror, removes her
underwear. Examines her thighs, plucks at a few hairs.
Slowly her breasts appear, her belly, her hips. Slowly she
spills out her nakedness. Her feet contract, they tread on a
cold, uncarpeted floor.

She lies down.
Spreads her hair over the pillow. Looks at the plaster
ceiling, the books, the curtains that partially keep out the
morning light.

She curls up as if she were a nest. Stretches out and huddles
up again. Hides under the sheet.

Her womb is in her stomach. Her heart rests and beats in
her chest. All her limbs, her whole body, begin to settle
down, to sleep in their rightful place.

Her eyes scarcely open, scarcely look at the light bulb
hanging from a naked cord, the photos on the walls behind
which life continues.

She covers her eyes with the sheet. Uncovers them. Looks at
me from under heavy eyelids. "Why is it," she says, "that I
need you more when I feel most alone? Our desires seem to
come from a part of us which has died."

The muffled honk of a horn penetrates.

A man beyond the door is talking to someone, explaining to
a tiny female voice.

We can hear steps going down the stairs, labored breathing
fades away.

In the room next door a glass object falls to the floor.
Persephone shivers.
Puts her hands over her face like a mask.
Her sleepy eyes look at me without looking.
Dawn weighs her whole body down.
"Persephone."
"Turn off the light."
Your light, my light, all the light.
There's too much sun, an excess of stars.
Even antipoets and assassins have a cranny of light. Even in
an idiot's foggy memory the radiance of a kind afternoon
persists.
I want to sleep. She chuckles under the sheet in the
penumbra she contrives.

"Persephone."
She doesn't answer. Forsakes me for her sleep, for her
well-being.
Abandons me to the solitary ceremony.
She begins to sleep while others put on their bodies like
jackets, to live all over again like insects who thrive on the
sun by day and die from darkness and cold at night.
Her brassiere, her earrings, her feet, her dress are resting.
Her handbag on the chair looks like an old woman's face.
Objects seem to speak in their dumbness, acquire human
form.

If she dreams the whole creation dreams.
Knowing and remembering fly on the same wing.
Light, darkness become visible, hold back in her eyes.
Things take shape in accordance with her being.

• • •

She lies there curled up in an *h,* submerged like a fish in its element.
While the others carry on, while the others shout.
Business is done. There is talk of contracts, of teeth, of sunglasses, of houses without windows, of men without legs. They make speeches, dedicate fountains, wave to right and left, are photographed next to a plaque or an orphan.

She lies there, distant from the hour that lives in her.
But there's still time to bestir her, to tell her that with me she can glimpse a dawn that doesn't appear by night or by day.
That my greatest desire is to see us immersed in one of ourselves until she speaks my words that speak her, my desires that seek her out in her lack of desires,
that we must do it before sleep, before she awakens, and before the brothel takes her away and encapsulates her in an atmosphere of prostration.

But she's already asleep.
And tomorrow I won't have the conviction to tell her.
So I smoke, shut in with her absence in the darkened room.
And I can't see the smoke. I only feel the solidity of the chair, which might not be there, which could be the table or the frigid glare of the mirror, or could be her dream covering me with objects.

And I can't wake her up, perhaps because of an absurd fear that it wouldn't be her, that it would be the prostitute I've passed many times in the street as I hurried by, that it would be the beggar who touched my face making signs over my eyes with her gaunt hands;

that she would have another face, that her face would be a
piece of sheet with holes in it;
that it would be her, but she wouldn't recognize me,
wouldn't see me;
and also, because I've known women who've looked at me
with hatred when I woke them up, who've broken something
forever, since I let them see my real face in that moment of
confused lucidity.

I give a lot of thought these days to what can be done
during working hours. I draw up lengthy itineraries in which
everything comes out as planned, once the traps are laid
where she will run aground, unaware of the capture or the
snares, due to the vehemence of the siege, or its
transparency.
But I can't wake her up.
She is overwhelmed by gravity.
Seeing her sleeping face is like being asleep.
I see the dampness of her temples, of her hair falling in
distinct locks over the bedspread.
I see her dark nostrils. Her lips pressed against each other.
I see her hands, her arms extending down the bed, as if her
whole body were supported by crutches.
I see her pallid cheeks, bloodless in the flaccidity of sleep.
I see her body as a stain, above which clarity and the night
harmonize.

I hear her breathing resounding here and everywhere, as if
her body were the world's lung.
I hear her footsteps, as if her feet were walking tirelessly
along the streets of the world.
I hear the sweat trickling over her.

. . .

I see a glass of water for a thirsty girl fresh from the fields,
who is full of distances, of ever-changing suns that make the
gaze tremble;
a house, three steps up to the front door, a little bell rings,
the dogs bark, an old woman looks out of the window and
asks who's there in the voice of a deaf person.
I see water over Persephone's nakedness, bathing her,
cleansing her of memories, of stories she alone remembers,
of feelings she alone knows have been lost.
The water from before we got ready to make love, from after
we had made love; tepid and weightless above still tremulous
skin.
The water that finds us weary of rubbing our nakedness
together, our desire, the most intimate thing given to us, so
that we can consume it in haste.
The water that carries away weariness from sleepless eyes,
and the sight of stockings slowly removed.
The water I love and that loves her.

I see a fragment of night at the window, an intrusion of the
future or the past into the present.
Old clocks, fat criminals with politicians' faces, broken
objects in the closet.
I say words to myself. Prince. Child. Book. Cylinder. Flower.
Tree. Darkness. And I don't sleep.
The wardrobe is there, pious and solitary.
The furniture, the picture, the wall clock, the umbrella cover,
the china duck, the record player, the green cushion, the
lamp, the vase, the deck of cards, the curtains, the sweater,
the pair of pants, my ring, the socks, the shoes, the rag doll
are there.

In the cupboard there is salt, cans of tomatoes and soup,
rice, coffee, cinnamon, chocolate.
The time and the body I live in don't sleep, don't dream,
don't live what I want.

Inside this room there is a more private room which thinks
it has no walls; its name is Persephone.
Whitewashed stairs, white light, serene light, rosy whiteness
raise it up, surround it.
The sky is its ceiling; its corridors lead everywhere, come
from everywhere.
In its mirror I search for a soul resembling her, but it's
tarnished, and only objects come out of its plate glass, out of
its solid lake.
Sounds, fires, shadows come out. Out come
Susi, Marta and Magdalena. Out come
books, chess sets, stuffed birds, voices. Out come
empty wine bottles, cities, overexcited women. Out come
newspapers discarded in the street, adolescents and young
girls showing their thighs. Out come
memories of memories, eyes, which are mine, spying on
strangers, storefronts, closed windows, half-open doors,
eyelids that will never capture me because they no longer
exist.
Out they come, and nothing ever stops.

Everything comes down to the white bed, where my secret
aspirations roam; there we do everything forever.
Everything comes down to her aging skin, everything leads
to separation.

．　　．　　．

"You'll see for yourself," the salesman said heartily,
"hammocks give a touch of class to any garden, any balcony
that's big enough. They relax the muscles here, and here.
You can set them up anywhere. They're great in your
bedroom, a refuge, a hiding place, a way of getting away
from the world.
If you're not thinking of adding a garden to your home, if
you're not thinking of building right now,
you'll still find a use for it, you'll still enjoy it no matter
where you hang it.
That won't be a problem for you. You couples make your
nest to suit your immediate needs. You can always use them
as beds.
You can use them for thinking, if your brain wants to.
Also, one or the other can use it for a rest, for an occasional
vacation from compulsory conjugal company.
The atmosphere they make for themselves, the little escapes
from routine, have a lot to do with young couples' morale.
If you don't like this one we can look at some others that
have a special print. A design of birds and flowers, with
houses and trees. In short, nature in your home, in a
hammock.
You know, vulgarity begins with ordinary furniture. The
price of distinction is minimal. Just spend a little money, but
spend it well.
Believe me . . . Just for the pleasure of seeing such a nice
couple in one of these hammocks, I would gladly give it to
you. But inside this modest stomach there are imperious
needs. And so, just as my belly grows, and not because of
blooming pregnancy, everything goes up . . . handsome
young people."

                    .   .   .

But it's not enough to throw yourself like a bundle into a
hammock to be happy.
Dark and bright corridors open out beyond a hammock.
Imagination and forgetting hover above someone who lies
down in a hammock to look at the sky.
Gladness and dread mesh under the witness to an exodus of
birds and clouds.
A blue well falls without falling over the eyes of whoever
lies there, amazement covers his face.
Birds of prey fight on the wing over his soul.
He must sleep with his eyes open to infinity. He must not
become plunder for the devious hawk who waits for the
moment when he will rise to the bird's beak.

Persephone is sleeping.
I make signs with my fingers over an enraptured face above
her face. I free her being from the ceiling, the walls, the
door. I see her framed by a blissful nimbus.
I recreate her eyes, which took on different tones the first
time I embraced her.
I ring a bell over her chest as a harbinger of her sacred
night.
I slide in by her side, feeling I am someone else.
I take her face between my hands as if it were a crystal ball,
and I look into it.
In her face I see a short trip through small villages, black
butterflies in her path, fields of rain, squashed crickets.
Adobe houses, green silences, a drop of blue like an eye in
the infinite, a cloudy night sky like a blind man whose eyes
are only for crying.
Dissolute mouths, songs that drown out words, smother sobs.
Cages, red clay pots, butchers' stands, lights in public

squares, hotels, hearts inflamed with rage and about to
explode.
I see, and I remember, and I know that in one single instant
these revelations will give meaning to all things forever.
I remember, and I know why, when her bag was snatched in
the market, I felt a certain solidarity with the thief.

But things only exist in their own time, and, with rare
exceptions, the confidence needed for action lasts only as
long as the effort it required, and what we thought was
lasting is ended almost imperceptibly and without last rites,
and the pain we fear is not the pain it should have caused
us, but a different one, the pain of not being able to feel it,
of facing situations we've already lived through. Because
pain can only exist in our memory, within that orbit of
obsolete beings and things known to have lost their time.
But that's enough.
I've left thousands of trees behind, I've passed thousands of
people on streets and highways, in museums and parks and
stores,
and I end up asking myself: What good is so much time,
what good is so much death?

And I said to her: "Make a poem."
And she showed me the roundness of a breast.
(Afterwards she gave me a few vulgar lines.)

And the wave: flip-flop: burns.

Moreover we have to reach noon, our colleagues busy
outside, the good people shut up at home.

Without recognizing each other or saying goodbye, swimming
in our loose clothing, without having unnecessary dreams
beneath the cloudy December sky. Because we can't stand so
much hope, so many images in the air, such cold under the
hidden sun.
Surviving without surviving.
Attending the funerals of ministers and country bumpkins.
Shifting words around for a more explicit construction.
Protesting crimes against saints and rabble.
Hoisting up the day as if it were really ours.

We'll talk afterwards, we'll find warm words to speak of
what we don't and would like to have.
With a hundred words bubbling up at once to name one
single unessential article, we'll keep on talking tirelessly
until we've emptied ourselves out, until we have nothing else
to say to each other.

We'll talk about Barbara and Beatriz, about two separate
bodies sharing one reality.
We'll see them looking at us, smiling at us, winking coldly
from afar. And we will pass from stare to stare.
Thinking that they are the ones who leave on night trains, at
the hour that strikes.

And we will go on talking until we are alone again, far
removed from impressions and memories,
trying to find ourselves a place in the rejoicing, a farewell in
the air, a being for love and time to find out what is
happening to us.

Until our presence no longer disturbs, no longer forces
movement on this landscape lost forever;
until our minds no longer worry themselves searching for
and weaving traces.

We will turn off the light, we will turn it on many times in
many situations, with different people and different ourselves.
Nothing will be lost or gained, except what we were able to
keep, what we would have liked to hold captive and for
ourselves, what flutters on the wall, on the curtains, and is
far away.

But then, what's the purpose of these lines being written—
and erased once they are read— of the shadow's trembling
with fear, of nudity that emerges but doesn't converge, of the
calm that seeks us out, of the experience that could
transform us, if life is killing us when it is, and also kills us
when it doesn't move us as we want it to.

This is what I always say to myself one way or another when
I'm walking along the street or when, at times, I live only
through thought.
This is what always sends me back to dubious places, where
memory distorts and fragments an indivisible experience.
This is what always happens to me when I talk at night,
when I have long conversations with strangers and mumble
vague coherencies and lost desires.

I have lived in two monsters, the one who says yes and the
one who denies me.
I have thought about an exchangeable and elastic body.
I have witnessed stupidity sound by sound, in all its colors.

I have felt happiness in someone's laugh, and I have
squeezed it at its most fragile part, until I could see its blood
and the substance of which it is made.
I have drunk normality and excess from a woman, I have
cursed in the middle of her ecstasy, in the middle of our
embrace, in the middle of myself.
I have chosen limbo over birth in the dungheap, even
though I dream of, I live in that dog groaning amongst the
garbage.

Persephone sleeps on. She is not here. But she is not at rest.
A cry spurts from the place where she lies.
Its echo settles on the armchair, the mirror, so I can see how
suffering yawns audibly, and how a single woman can
torment herself and rain down black rain;
so we can doubt even ourselves, and wonder why it doesn't
end and keeps on echoing blindly off the furniture;
wonder why Sonia's cry flowers in this one, when she's
already been buried and gone down in her white dress to
sample the density of the unknown.

Persephone smiles in her sleep.
Sonia can go, crawl, grieve in immateriality.
It's gotten late everywhere, children are old men, decaying
mingled dust; the innocents of those days now revel in the
smells of contact.
All past weeping is in the fog, and Sonia has lost her uses,
her fingernails.

Long ago I watched that young girl with pointy breasts grow
up loving me, day after day hint at a meeting with her flesh.
When I used to return at dawn she would open her door

wordlessly, her shadow barely visible at the center of her bedroom.

I never entered.

I would go straight to my room and fall asleep thinking about what she was thinking.

The next day we would say hello as if she had never opened her door, as if she hadn't offered me what flowered between her thighs.

She died on a Monday. They took her away quickly to the cemetery. During the funeral her father told me she was his brother's daughter, and that he had been nothing more than her mother's inept brother-in-law.

We returned discussing the fate of virgins in the beyond.

When the brothel's owner dissolves at the borders of an abhorrent space and becomes nothing more than an empty brothel in the daylight.

When Susi sleeps unknown to all, and the man who slobbers lengthily on her back has covered her with fetid breath and sperm.

When our hotheaded brothers slash the air with vehement gestures, assassinate someone on a street corner, and the middle-class wife tries on her wig, tightens her belt before stepping into the street.

When those who were transfixed by terror during the night see the ghost become smaller than a grain of darkness.

When I, nose, mouth, eyes, feel day licking my neck, without finding anyone at the bottom of my dream, without finding her at the edge of her body.

When there is neither voice nor sound to describe what is happening inside us,

the abomination waits and dreams in the brothel, its irreverent geometry shrouds immodest nymphs with slender feet, multiplied naked and painted within dark walls;

foul-smelling dampness calls out in the corners, as if signaling the absence of any fertility, of any meager light;

on the musicians' stage the instruments and chairs die a slow death, are abandoned by fate, hint at dissipation;

there's a hidden, coiled shadow in every object weighing on
the floor;
the beds that foresee the traces of eventual bodies lie there
like traps that must muddle the meaning of every birth, the
future of a man or of a halfhuman whelp;
the souls of fulfilled desires moan in my memory, gratuitous
acts like zeros, anxiety that hasn't found a way out and
becomes embittered awaiting its chance.

Day converges into a chilly radiance; the words spoken by a
man in the street open up a strange fusion of warmth and
vitality in the entrenched winter.
The moth on the windowpane is a survival of yesterday, an
omen. The gossamer city seems to fly tenuously, without any
impelling force.

But Susi and Marta intrude above and below the present
hour, dance, chatter.
The owner desperately tries to take shape in the smoke of
the cigarette I crush on the floor.
Persephone is standing up, dressed in red, her eyes
provocative, her mouth kindled and her breasts provocative,
three steps away from the floozie, who is just about to . . .
say goodbye forever to some part of herself, thanks to an
excess of alcohol.

I see Persephone dauntlessly acquiescing, mulling over the x,
y and z of what shouldn't be done, allowed, taken personally
or become a habit.
Lulled by the buzzing rhythm, suggesting to the visitor who
lies there waiting that he can rub in several different ways or
from a single traditional and effective position.

Opening out in yawns, thighs and hips at the passing of
sticks wearing pants, shirts and shoes.
Showing her most secret face, the one that never appears in
my arms and that she practices carefully in the mirror, the
one I thought I loved, when it's precisely the one I haven't
been able to possess;
when she places herself between desires and the hunger for
them, between the musicians' splutterings and the puffed up
prostitutes who contort themselves and laugh;
between those who argue stubbornly over a drop of someone
and those who put their arms around the first waist that
comes near;
between the confused clamoring about sperm, tequila and
women and the red shadow of a waiter, a man, an object;
between those who don't know how to smile or banter and
those who produce a twanging in the air, a brittle gabbling,
a joke told by rote and bungled;
between the partying crowd and those who feel abandoned
by their mother, their lover or the light itself.

I see a pair of pants stained by the intensity of Persephone's
movements; I see the pornographic inspiration the drawings
above the beds provide, the wine and cigarettes on black
trays, the doors that lock from the inside and are opened
with dollar bills;
the whores' out-of-tune singing;
the whores' obscene gestures;
the possibility of a crime, of a double extinguishing of
consciousness; my project for changing her idea of the
world, her sense of mobility, her perception of words and
colors.

.   .   .

I see her grave without flowers or epitaph.
Her gradual subterranean diminution, her bony emptiness,
her unconscious transformation into dust, into others' chance
recollections, into stories told at parties by people neither
alive nor dead, into thistles trampled or uprooted by the
gardener.
I see her totality, her circle, her letter, her number;
her horse-, island-, star-shape, her girl-shape which can be
drawn and erased from the blackboard.

I cohabit her cohabitation.
I feel how they stroke her name, her thighs, her neck.
I hear the things they murmer into her ear.
I look at the expression of the multiple, trembling man, the
zeal in his eyes that want to plunge in, his confused words
that want to plunge in, his shoes that want to plunge in.
I hear the noise of his ego as he pulls down zippers and
skirts and stockings and bodies which can always go farther
down.
I see her being solicitous, pleasant, her heavy breasts
swaying as she walks, as she straightens out the rug that
gets in her way,
intuitively knowing what her adversary, the customer, is
thinking,
guessing at what he feels but doesn't say.
I follow her, suffocated, in her junction.
In her inquisitorial ardent movements.
In her feet, separated from each other and touching the
sheet.
In her legs, twined around the other body.
I look at her face, the dispersion of her hair,

the ceiling she looks at without seeing it,
the closed window,
the curtains.
I pretend not to know that she enjoys it, that she surrenders
to the other and enjoys it, that she feels pleasure away from
me.
I watch her in her vertigo, when her past and future are
reduced to sex and they moan during orgasm.
I even watch her afterwards, still holding the man's body in
her arms, the thick root between her thighs:
moist and nuptial, unable to say a word.
Until she pushes aside the burden weighing her down;
observes herself fondly in the mirror,
smokes a cigarette,
gathers her clothes,
full of world,
full of many consecutive beings.

She's awake now by my side, her face and the bed immersed
in light, her hands folded over her chest.
Opening her eyes, breathing here and now, asking me if I'm
asleep, if I slept, when she sees that my eyes are open.
Going off again. Opening her eyes again. They're so lustrous
they seem to shimmer; her chin juts out over the sheet and
her fingers clutch the edges.

The instant that makes me believe she is next to my body is
lying. Or I'm deceiving myself when I see her smiling at me.
She is by my side elsewhere.
She's inside her own memory, skating alone over days gone
by, now happy days, because they're dead.

In a park she watches a butterfly, which she'll come across
several twilights later pinned to a table in a disreputable
hotel.
Back home she talks to her mother about her future as the
wife of a young man agile as a dream.
The night of her birthday she trembles because a boy
touched her breast, made her feel the elasticity of her soul,
the shivers of her bodily constellation.
She discusses with her friends the wisdom of feigning a
fragile love with men, a controlled ardor, a provocative
disdain.
She is with the man who rubbed at her painstakingly until
he deflowered her, and never even said hello or goodbye
after the inauguration,
when it was necessary, because she was walking alone in the
street, because she was alone in the café, or sitting next to
him in the classroom.
She returns to him, seeking a repetition, a faithful
continuity.
But only for a few months, since later she would realize that
all men can make love.
She's naked, in different countries, entrusting the greatest
part of her being to the mirror.
She is lost as the days are lost, in round intimate hours,
feeling the pulse of beings and things which are hard to put
into concrete form, and not into a yawn or a bored flick of
her fingers.
Something about her becomes arbitrary, an interior landscape
shaped by her whim, or simply natural association of
memory.
She breathes far in the past, and her present is already over.

·　·　·

The objects that make me believe in her presence lie. The
surroundings that envelop her in a time which is not
contemporaneous to her lie. The mirror which reflects her
image lies.
She is floundering in some brothel, in some forgotten
anecdote, in some incident.
A mournful horizon revolves before her eyes.
An afternoon, an embrace, a wave smother her.

Whiteness clothes the windowpanes, gives a halo and weight
to objects.
Things vibrate as light skims over them.
Noon rustles the curtains.
Persephone unfolds like a narrow, steep staircase.
She sits down on her soft cushions. Sits down on a bed
whose wrinkled covers form a rudimentary throne.
She puts her elbows on her knees, her head in her hands
She looks at me like tinder menaced by fire.

My hands stroke her limbs. The paleness of her skin and the
redness of her passion mottle her arms and legs.
The same warmth enlivens her heart, her feet, her fingers.
The fire opens up her body, like a conflagration discovering
many windows, many eyes in a house.
As if she had turned herself inside out, and a private color
swept over her nuancing her features.

My senses awaken.
I hear my body, I hear her body become entangled in mine.
Both grow, ripen, wither, die.
I hear the echo of their disappearance, of their birth.
I hear. That they arrive, that they depart.

I feel her body. It touches my body through a thousand open pores. Grazes me with a thousand hands and thighs, with flesh that parts like lips.

I smell her source. Her desire. Her ashes.

Her hair damp from my hair. Her caress that is my caress.

I see the word she doesn't say on her curved tongue, arching towards mine. Her sex that imprisons mine. Her outstretched feet. The movement of her hips making sparks fly from the sheets. Her body subsiding into the mattress. Her rising and falling and noise. The momentary darkness of her mouth.

An arm fills my field of vision. An eye. A thigh. A span of stomach. Her hair. Her navel.

Her face turned to the right. Her face turned to the left. Her chin pointing upwards and pointing downwards. Her contracted body. Her diagonal body.

Her navel. Her ear. Her hair. Her mouth going in deeper and deeper, sinking inside her, falling and falling, touching my sex, climbing my body, becoming my mouth that kisses her mouth that goes in deeper, and falls into me, and falls into her.

Revolving absent and present in the firmness, in the softness, in the dampened hair, in the crushed breast.

Absent and present in touching and being touched, one foot in the absolute void.

Together and in tune fingers and lyre. Far off, at the very center, impossible to locate, of the wheel of a bicycle, going so fast the spokes have disappeared and in their place a sharp, ominous wind has sprung up.

I see her rounded, sunken glance go by. I see her eyelashes, brows and lids go by. Her half-open lips. Her breasts, tipped by small, pointed prominences. Her navel. Her nose.

Different faces pass before her face, brighten and darken. Greed, the sight of a shadow foundering while its master, the body, calmly leans back against the rocks, looking at another landscape, keep reappearing in the faces.

Which of all her faces is my face, which one will be waiting for me when the embrace is over, which one will keep my expression, my wedlock, my displacement? Or must they all vanish, so that when I awake I will see only a tired gesture which doesn't capture me fading from the mirror?

She slowly comes apart in my arms. She illuminates beings, bodies, clothes hanging that are phantoms, chairs that watch and are dumb, colors that breathe and sounds of skin, eyes that open in the past, in the present.
She grows and sighs among dreams that turn real and realities that become dreams. Love burns and blazes between her thighs. Smoke rises from her body.
She covers her face with my hands, covers my eyes with her hands.
She breathes like a horse beaten by the impatience of its own haste.
She rises above our bodies supported by her own body. Disappears into them. Wind. Rain. Earth. She comes back to us, is us, this body, this offering, this birth of man, this woman.
Her arms see, her hands hear, her gaze feels, her brain touches. Where she burnishes our skin there is light.
She has me kiss her breast. Kisses me as a way of kissing herself, of reaching her own breast.
I am a touch, a man, a desire. What I am, what Persephone

is, becomes knotted, sinks into the bed like a stone into water.

Instead of entering her, I seem to emerge from her.

Her love confines me like a niche.

I can breathe the afternoon at her center. I can feel the weight of a sunless hour and the stuffy air at the core of her being.

Noon leaves a trace of the unattainable in her, of remoteness, of what happened a long time ago.

I see the dark afternoon in her eyes, crisscrossed by troubled light whose wings are almost black.

The noises that prattle in the street and rattle the windows crash into silence as if they would break it.

Love kisses mutual desire with its hidden tongue.

It touches our hands with a double hand, touches our eyes confused by the double fusion.

It guides the movement that confirms us, the feeling, the flight, our scattered image.

It rocks like a ship, gentle as a river that meanders rippling between fish and misty trees, without knowing where it's headed, but knowingly.

Love makes us into a single beast, a gazelle whose motionless body is still in flight.

Love makes us into a flexible sword that bends from hilt to tip.

Love is like a wing that brushes a man's head above the water, like a snake's tongue flickering through a pore in the skin; it is the wine drunk by the drinker's desire, a hare which flees, a hawk that pursues.

. . .

Every instant has its own reality, its shadow, its sound, and
its share of color, maidenhood, fear and emptiness.
Beyond natural love is imaginary love, the immersion of the
image in the body, the immersion of the spirit in the
image.
Persephone's sweat sticks to my body like an embrace, the
smell and taste of her skin is my smell and taste. The flame
that moves inward and issues from the core of her body is
pure and diagonal.
No movement is in vain. All flesh, all doubt has its meaning.
Whether she comes near or she moves away, she is joined
to me. Submerged in submersion she is joined to me.
A few inches higher, a few inches lower, she is joined
to me.
She is oblation, offering and sustenance, the meaning within
meaning, breath within breath, gaze within gaze, inspiration
and expiration.

Her hands are in my hands, her feet in my feet, her
forehead in my forehead, her energy, her restlessness, the
being who flows indiscriminately through my energy or my
restlessness.
Her whispering lips, her clumsiness, her deep chamber, her
flesh, the momentary notion of her flesh, her rhythm, her
oppression.
Desire parts her lips. A narrow channel opens up beneath
her tongue. Fire and a captive silence burst out.
Something of hers enters. Something of hers departs. There's
life without interruption. She moves forward and backward
by half a word each second. Almost doesn't exist, barely
exists.
Her mouth is soft, her palate yielding. Her desire touches

what her imagination feels. Her voice, the murmuring of her voice, is present, is presence.

The more she burns the more she stokes the fire, dreams this external dream with me.

She approaches and runs away at the same time. She takes me in her arms, comes and goes like a narrow path that widens, like a surf in which no one will swim twice, like an island with two headlands.

Her mind runs with her senses, her consciousness quickens. She is born. Dies. Her womb is smoke. Her womb is dust. Her body is an embryo.

She acquires unity in my being. Appears in me in another shape.

She has many eyes, innumerable mouths. Repulsion lifts her up, attraction fastens her to me.

She disappears and reappears like a dream in which harmony keeps each thought, each image, each being in its place, in which the distance that separates them is equal to the affinity which draws them to a point where all distance is meaningless.

She laughs. Feels pleasure. Hurts. Does all this in a single moan. Moved in her depths, in every diameter of her skin which listens and knows it is sacred and ephemeral.

Her calm and her frenzy have a body. A real body that moves. She gives rein to memories, age to the present. Presses against me like a she-wolf. Opens up like a carniverous plant. Wounds my back with her nails.

My left arm is beneath her head. I penetrate her spaces, her time, her transition. I enter the time she promises and the time that is. I don't know if I'm going to her or she's coming to me.

. . .

She moves too slowly or too fast.

She seems to advance, although she is still. She seems born to the world in each gesture, in each movement, in her very stillness.

She grows, she spreads out, becomes deeper and deeper, more and less Persephone.

She sinks with her inhabitant, binds him, revolves around him.

Face down, she hardens her thighs. Arches her back.

Contracts when she should contract. Straightens out.

Face up, she shapes the man inside her sex, gives him countenance, image and memory. Death.

She delves farther into her own space, into painful chambers.

All her darkness advances, closes all eyelids, bolts, fists.

Her body is sanctuary, mouth and clothing.

My hands are touching clouds.

They touch arms, eyes, faces, stomachs stretched all over the world and my being.

In her thermal night I find my soul in its human form.

Her mouth is open and her eyes are moist as she propagates a new body, rids herself of the old one, is reborn in another, exhausts it, discards it. She gives novelty to each minute, constant initiation.

She tears out her unborn heart. Unfurls her entire being, draws it in, casts it again.

Leaves shadows behind her, shreds of us both.

She pushes with her breast, her stomach and her heart.

A glowing spark arcs from her body to my sex, from my sex to her body. All that germinates in her burns, all that burns

germinates. Everything she rubs against, everything she
kindles loves her.
A seminal liquor, a gentle friction, a tickling sensation
enliven her. Her body blazes from within, from her fissure.
There where the eye cannot see, where touch cannot enter,
there is where I enter her.
Her walls narrow, widen, launch a time of real ghosts.
Her hands and feet, her eyes and her faces are everywhere.
Her eyes seem to be spying on me rather than seeing me.

Breached, she kneels; leaves a warm imprint.
Her pendulous breasts graze the sheets. She holds her
reddened ear to the sound of the embrace.
Our desires—I think—are our ramparts.

Just as when we lose our bearings in a darkened room or in
too lofty flight, we float above the third member of our own
union.
We embrace like the branches above the stream entwine to
keep from falling, we interlace like the waters of a river that
curves around a bend.

Forgetting goes with momentary knowledge.
Out of every image we extinguish another emerges,
incorporating the previous one.
Breadth permeates height, abundance penetrates emptiness.
Something fluid brings us together, something that goes
before us, that stumbles, rights itself and continues.
Our rhythms are in phase. They rise, hover at midpoint,
descend.
Love inflames her cheeks as fire ignites the dry grass.
I dream inside her.

I see love beating among the shapes inside her.
I hear her warmth and flame inside her.
Suddenly she pauses. Like a woman who's afraid of taking
the easy way, and automatically seeks out the most arduous
paths.
She glides from her interior, shifts towards her center.
She hollows out her intimacy. Saturates the time, the place,
the body we inhabit with herself.
And she comes, tearing herself apart, consuming herself.

The permeable, hermetic day surrounds us and contains us,
grows inside us, has assumed the shape of things.
Nothing gives us away, except our dealings with the world,
what we call our world.
We gradually become indivisible from our memories, from
what we expect, from what we conceal, from what we are not.
Time flows out of a bird's beak, through a sound that can
pierce the most ludicrous human chimera as easily as a
flower.

Someone is staring at us from across the way. Whether man
or woman's, a pair of eyes shows up as a black speck over
there.
We can hear his breathing cross the street, become thin
enough to go through the walls, windowpanes, curtains. He
walks around the room insensibly, blends into us.
He wraps himself in light and shadow, but we never see his
body, or see him touch us, or move.
Flattened against the walls, buzzing around the light,
creeping with the spider which spies on us from the ceiling.
He was there before us, dressed in wall and window, in
womens' clothes, in colors.

He whispers his name inside us, but we cannot, we will not
say it yet ourselves.
He is an eye on our hands, more profound than the word
eye; he is a love so strange in our love that it's hard to
believe he is love.

I have grown to forget many things, but I always return, I
am at the same place, unconvinced.
All happiness lasts but a moment, and the time that follows
is only good for remembering what we have lost.
At night, after the rainy months, I have seen numbers and
letters peeling off a poster that seemed infinite.
I have seen traffic lights and street lamps and I was sure I
was walking elsewhere than on earth.
I have clarified hazy connections between fire and water,
between eyes and the sun, between a woman who no longer
exists and a woman standing on a street corner who looked
at me as if she recognized me when I walked by, as if I
should stop and ask if she had known the dead woman.
I have called total strangers by spontaneous names, and they
have smiled at me as if remembering a past complicity or a
future meeting, and I, too, have remembered and turned my
back on them.
I have walked straight ahead along many streets, certain that
I would meet up with my double on the last one, and when I
was almost at the end I closed my eyes, turned my head and
looked at my shadow, and I thought that if I were to see
another body and another shadow looking at me, I would not
suffer a fatal blow, but my own disappearance.
I have wished for our transference into each other through
love, but at the climax of my doubling I have glimpsed the

void that separates us, and the vertigo I felt made me vomit
and faint into that caesura between bodies.

How obtuse is the little person here by my side who is
recalling the days, who spins and unravels them in her
pedestrian way, who winks, who makes categorical
statements while savoring the caresses of a long-gone lover
between her thighs.
How obtuse is this greedy, incarnate stupidity.
How obtuse is this horizon, so suited to her charms, this
soliloquy that endlessly says her name.
I would like to banish her from this encapsulated landscape,
if there was any other reality as viable for my soul as her
body's.

The day is crepuscular and so is the bourgeois, gnawing at
his food and at his children's necks.
The party dress put away in the closet, time being buried by
the clock, the dream in which we hope to take shelter are
crepuscular.
The face yawning in the street is crepuscular, and the mirror
that reflects a faded armchair.
The verses I remember to exorcise the pain of another
memory are crepuscular.
God and women and the silent demon who hides behind the
screens to watch copulation are crepuscular.

Persephone's shoulders are heavy on my chest. Lying on her
back on top of me, she stretches her hands out. Her loose
hair hangs from my chin like a silky animal.
Her body is straight, her head still.

She presses her skull against my mouth, against my lips
covered by her hair.

I kiss her neck, but she seems not to notice my kiss, or my
arms encircling her beneath her breasts; she seems not to
notice my legs and my feet.

A gray atmosphere begins to rise inside me, to invade and
weigh on my eyelids.

My body shrinks, disappears, leaving only two eyes that
stare at the mirror as if it were cold, petrified water.

Her head feels far away, absent between my arms clasping
her like a necklace above her stomach.

The smell, the taste of her hair suddenly make me feel
nauseous, physically weary, apprehensive of a vacant future.

The mirror recedes until it almost becomes liquid,
insubstantial and permeated with blue fog.

My hands touch only emptiness, as if her body was no
longer there, as if it had evaporated.

The light that filters in through the curtains, creating an
artificial twilight in the room, dazzles me.

An awareness that ages everything, that ages me,
overwhelms me.

As I close my eyes I see her face staring at me maliciously.

I open my eyes with difficulty, I see her motionless head
turned toward the window.

I ask her if she turned around to look at me, but my voice
is so dull and weak that she doesn't answer.

I press hard against her stomach, to make sure she's still
there, hasn't gone anywhere.

I keep up the pressure. I do it again, to make her react.
But she doesn't look round. She doesn't move, as if she
wasn't the woman I'm touching.

As if I was only touching a deserted body which gets heavier
and heavier, leans increasingly against me, becomes colder.

I look at the mirror; it's icy and vaporous, as if someone had
deposited all her vapor and ice there,
by dint of kissing it all over with damp lips,
by pressing skin covered with lips against it;
I look at the table, at the objects impregnated with
fingerprints,
as if a many-handed creature had marked them to the core
with its desolation.
I look at the floor, the ceiling, the walls
plastered with yellowish and black sweat, with traces of
human feet,
sweating a dampness that bubbles out, that seems to stand
up, to have a life of its own.
I look at Persephone's head, her neck, her hair brushing my
chin, falling on my chest, and her body feels chill and
clammy.
I try to close my eyes again, to find the dream I want and
can't find.
My eyelids squeeze against my brain, which won't leave off
thinking.
She looks me in the face, goes right through me.
I get up from the bed, dislodging her body without realizing
it.
I look at the mirror again, at the table, the ceiling and the
walls. But they are dry, without a vestige of dampness or
cold.
She is lying down, asleep with her eyes open, warm.
I lie down next to her, cover her shoulders with the blanket,
prepare to sleep.

I am slowly dwindling, cradling myself. A room, a bed are
once again my first world.

I feel the cool sheet, white and protective.

I smile, like someone among familiar beings who cannot hide
his happiness, even though he assumes a mature, grave voice
when speaking to them.

The curtains are backlighted. The cream-colored ceiling
recedes, approaches.

The departing train penetrates the room with a husky noise.
A honking horn makes the windows rattle.

Voices from the street argue in counterpoint, then fade away.
Embroidery on the bedspread glitters like a fat, blue bird.

My memory brings me lecherous gestures, parted thighs,
nipples rubbed short of bleeding.

I search for a little girl's face, a pen, an inkwell, the gilded
cardboard wings twitching on a schoolgirl's back at her
graduation.

I think of beings who are more image than substance.

I see a green house which has no doors or windows, only
walls and a roof.

A red tree in which Persephone climbs higher and higher, as
the foliage becomes more luxuriant and the crown grows
until it touches the clouds.

I rise with the tree that becomes taller and broader and
bluer.

I climb up, and when I look down I see Persephone, whom I
had almost reached, falling like a dead bird whose
arms-wings are broken.

Swiftly I descend with the tree until I touch the ground, but
I can only find a colored print of her being, a sheet of paper
her height stuck to the earth.

I try to lift her off the ground of which she has become a part.
To peel off the colored drawing in which she stamped herself. But I can only get pieces of her feet and her head.
I try to pick her up, and she disintegrates, and tears like a decal gummed to a window, while something moans in the air and something cries in her eyes.

She stirs on the bed.
Awkwardly pushes a lock of hair off her face, rubs her eyebrows, feels her cheeks as if gauging their warmth.
She makes an effort to recognize me, to become conscious of herself. Still slumbrous.
Her face has the rosy color induced by deep sleep. Her hands look thinner, paler, more tapered.
She smiles. As if she had finally seen and pondered over me.
She swings her feet off the bed. Part of the sheet goes with them, swaddling them in white wrappings.
She's still looking at me. Taciturn. Sitting on the edge. As if she didn't feel sufficiently awake to take a step.
She smiles again, stands up.
Goes towards the bathroom. Her nightgown clings to her body in places.
She closes the door.

I hear her turning on a faucet.
Washing herself.
Her face. Maybe. Her hands.
I hear her lifting the toilet seat.
Her intermittent urine.
I listen for a few seconds.
Or minutes.

Nothing.

I hear the faucet being turned on again.

Hands rubbing.

A towel thrown to the floor.

She comes back.

Her hands and face are clean, cool.

Her eyes look about alertly, avidly.

Her nightgown hangs at her waist.

Her breasts sway heavily from side to side.

She stops near me.

Says to me,

"Look."

She steps out of her nightgown as if it were a skirt.

Now she is naked.

Once again she says,

"Look."

I look.

Her breasts that point toward the floor.

So much use and misuse has modified them. So much
fondling and movement, so many fingers of love feeling her
heart beat have sloped them downwards.

She quickly gets into bed. Is seized by an intense shivering.

She gives me a hasty kiss. Turns her back to me.

The nightgown remains on the floor, a silky stain, a
transparent, deflated armor.

The tubes of her stockings dangle fleshily over the chair.

I kiss her back. Her neck. I feel how they get warmer.

My lips skim over her arms.

I return to her head as to the surface of a solid impenetrable
sphere.

I mumble a tune. More the music than the words.

My voice is so off-key that I fall silent.

.   .   .

The afternoon deposits its luster on the armchairs. Mantles doors and windows. Clings to the walls. Touches ground. Walks.

The chessmen are on the board, awaiting who knows which subsequent right movement, created for impersonal rites, suspended in the twentieth move by white's imminent downfall, for the king of whiteness can no longer choose and black must decide the maneuver that will accomplish the cataclysm elegantly.

Black has definitively invaded the enemy monarch's fastness through the successful intrigues of a bishop established on a solitary square and supported by the magic *L* of a knight who appears to be sleeping, wrapped up in himself.

White has no defense left, except to rush headlong into rash heroics, into a fatal brilliance, whose only glory, whose only prowess would be surrender in the middle of an inopportune combination.

A wooden dawn slowly rises from these defeats, peopled by the multiple ghosts of castles and kings, while an incorporeal bird breaks the silence in that tree, and a natural music seems to exist as pure matter.

The instants follow each other, an hour crumbles, pretending to perpetuate itself in a day which we know is ephemeral. A cloud skids by. A dog's barking thins out, runs quickly down the street.

Persephone raises her hands to her hair, and each word is already lost from the start, although it trembles.

Many distinct shadows make up a gray bestiary in gray metamorphosis in the sky, give a sense of fog, of a rainy season, of burgeoning, of enchantment.

. . .

The chessmen gleam in their immobility of stuffed warriors, ever ready to be sent to their thousandth death even though they have only lived momentarily in the lucid coherence of a man's system.
The white king no longer has any defense or chivalry; he hopes for an illusory salvation in the midst of a square wilderness, as if the chessboard's inflexibility would tolerate the empty gesture of a past mistake and the knight abandoned in a useless province could, in a single jump, fly over the abyss of the four *L*'s which have separated him from prostration and ashes since nine chimeras ago.
The white queen, discretely isolated by the enemy pawns who scornfully surround her, cannot and will not be able to go to the rescue of the white kingdom's precarious, humiliated honor, gradually ruined by the scant humanity of its strategy.
Meanwhile I am sure that the losers are remembering how their last bishop fell because of the incongruency of his reasoning.

Persephone looks at me, but in her exhilaration fails to understand how women can interrupt a fantasy or an extraordinary vision, if it is they who incite them with their originality and radiance.
I arrest the flight of her hand in the air, I recall other flights, other fruits of the body.
While the instants follow one another, and a stuttering hour passes, almost dead by now, almost beyond the morning which as children we thought was eternal.
At the moment in which I remember the landscape, shadow and sound that light struck from this body, which now gets

up from my side, its bare back and long hair sending me
after another recollection, in a funeral place that is not ours
but that memory retains and suddenly illuminates in a fixed,
irreparable image.
Persephone smokes her first cigarette, leaning back in bed.
She twitches the pinky of her left hand through an opening
in her nightgown between her breasts and her navel, as if
scratching herself.

A murky light touches the carpet, the closed curtains, shades
her thighs.
An undergarment on the chair resembles a sleeping bird.
The room is pervaded by an arid penumbra, the embrace of
two lights in the air.
There are pomegranates and nuts on the table; on the pillow
is the soft hollow left by her head. Two withered flowers, of
a spiteful green, lean against the rim of an empty bottle.
A seascape on the blue wall. Ochre seagulls wheel beneath a
stormy ochre sky. Two fisherman lounge doltishly on the
beach, surrounded by dead fish. At the shoreline a
flesh-colored dog drinks from a tide pool. A ship sails
silently into the distance.

There's a touch of rain in the air filtering into the room, a
hint of failure, a sterility.
The light on the windowpane is no longer the afternoon light
but the reflection of the glowing light bulb.
The alarm clock rings. I get up to turn it off. It stops
ringing. We hear shoes treading deliberately, like armor. We
hear water running from a faucet and a woman's voice
intermingled. In the apartment next door they are

hammering nails into the wall. They break an object, glass, by the sound of it.

They blow their noses and start to talk.

Persephone gets up from the bed. She walks like a pregnant woman within weeks of giving birth.

Her tongue sticks out slightly.

Her breasts graze the clothes she's poking through.

She transfers clothing from one place to another. Drops some on the bed. Puts her hand on her hip. Thinks. Or I believe she thinks.

Throws away her cigarette.

Goes into the bathroom.

Leaves the door open behind her thighs, her bare heels.

I follow her.

Either to see her or to bathe with her.

She looks at me.

Hugs herself as if she were cold.

Waves her hand at me. Runs the water. Moist steam drifts from the showerhead towards my face.

She's next to the tub.

An insect falls into the water that's accumulating; we see how it drowns, how its gilded wings and its body float, a pale, inert speck.

She slams the door in my face.

Yells "Idiot" at me.

The room fluctuates between daylight and electric light. A flash of lightning flirts at the window. The chairs, the bed and the wardrobe are dusty and gray.

I hear the shower running. I feel a body lowering itself into the tub.

I can see the plastic curtain, the blurred mirror.

. . .

Women wearing coats were coming out of the movie theatre.
They had glossy cheeks and expressions.
Up above, giant letters announced the movie premiere.
A shabby old hunchback was pacing back and forth.
A girl was primping her hair, darting her blue eyes to right
and left. She smiled incessantly.
Men and women dressed in black were crossing the
threshold of an old church. They were whispering, scowling
at each other.
A whore paused as two men called to her.
"I can take you both on," she said in an offhand way, barely
moving her lips.
A few drops of rain fell on our heads.
A young man hurrying by blew me an "I love you."
Persephone said goodbye when we turned the corner.

Black smoke was streaming from a factory into the sky.
The seething air of a summer noon was suffocating, even got
under the nails of a fat woman who stopped every ten feet to
catch her breath and wipe off the sweat.
Two men had tied a string of empty tin cans to a scrawny
dog's tail and were urging it to run.
A frail, white-haired lady protested timidly. The men gave
in, stroked the dog's head . . . and poked him and shouted
so loudly and fiercely that the animal disappeared like a
flash into the distance.
The lady seemed to blush.
The men snickered, but paid her their respects before going
on their way.
The honk of a horn rushed a group of children to the
sidewalk.

They grinned triumphantly at each other, and hinting and
pointing towards the behind of the mannish woman who was
steering them, ran around the corner.
The white-haired lady looked one last time at the place
where the dog had been, before opening the street door to
her room.

And the man who was arriving was me.
I see myself entering the brothel: longhaired cathouse.
The big room.
Notes played by beardless musicians were drifting off the
stage.
I wandered from table to table. The prostitutes called after
me, saying, "Hey, kiddo, want me to warm you up? Want
me to wake you up?"

I drink a beer. Smoke.
Walk around.
Dance with a middle-aged woman.
The big room is dim.
I spend money on her.
Then she goes off with someone else.
I discover Persephone's bored, calculating expression. Her
gray gaze, her gestures.
She is drinking with a stranger. She looks at me on the sly.
She drinks. Fastens her gray stare on me.
Comes towards me. Takes me by the hand, smiles at me.
We dance.
She hardly moves.
Breathes lightly.
The stranger tries to cut in.
She ignores him.

We go on dancing beneath the red penumbra.
We tell each other our names.
The gray gaze floats.
The stranger waits, disguised in fog, invisibility, inexistence.
We can guess at what he thinks he's looking at, but we don't
see it.
The customers, the whores come and go, hug each other,
kiss, make noise, fight over trifles.
The brothel, ringed by windows that only admit a mournful
gloom, resembles in its stony mirth a spider riddled by the
night.

I look at and listen to Persephone, the ragged tenderness of
her odd patience, the weary but elusive note to her slowness,
the fawning desire in her absence of desires.
I pursue, in spite of her, that calm, that fire, that evasive
form, that perception which apparently doesn't perceive.
I decide to take her away with me, to cross the hour, to
cross the night, to place her in a beginning, to place myself
in her beginning, to intertwine the threads.
We stand motionless in a corner, leaning against a column,
not speaking, listening to a dialogue between two whores so
alike they almost cancel each other out.
The penumbra recedes through the windows towards the city.
The city looms in a multiple blotch of lights.

After hugging and whispering into each other's ears, the two
whores glance at us, move apart and, without looking back,
make a hurried promise to meet again.
Within the diameter where they stood I see Persephone's
naked body, in an imaginary and imperious birth of her self.
The stranger still waits, breathing ever nearer. The tips of

his shoes gleam for an instant in a ray of light. A cigarette
burns between his lips.

A group of customers summon six whores, sit them on their
laps, feel them up from knees to breasts; the whores laugh.

The musicians prance and sing, they stamp their feet, they
all stare at someone, as if they were singing for that person
alone.

A drunkard collapses with a leaden groan, and a chair and
two glasses follow him; his skull cracks as it hits the floor.

A friend emerges from the penumbra, from the orphaned,
anonymous crowd. His eyes light up when he spots me.

He walks toward me confidently; mechanically and without
pausing begins to tell me about pseudoesoteric real events,
about the peculiar questions two customers asked him.

He laughs as he recounts his answers, the drawings he made
to illustrate them: what Achilles' shield was like, Solomon's
temple, the numerous and prophetic ziggurats.

Persephone looks elsewhere, at the shadows moving around
us, at beings who beckon and threaten just by looking.

I feel her unclasping her hand from mine, I hear the beat of
her impatience.

I hear words, dates, book titles, stories, memories, all
sounding like irrelevant noise.

I see a taciturn and unfeeling Persephone moving a few
steps away, closer to the waiting stranger.

I hear that monotonous, relentless, self-assured voice holding
forth, visiting labyrinths, witticisms and myths, in which
there seems to be some connection between snails, the wind,
zero and light.

A whore whistles to the musicians' rhythm, straddling a
chair backwards, her sex staring out. Her vague eyes vaguely
follow the curls of smoke.

The stranger takes Persephone by the arm, draws her to his
chest, encircles her waist, kisses her on the neck, on the
chin, while she looks at me.
Three customers wrangle with a heavy, broad-hipped girl,
push her into a corner, slap her, tug at her blouse.
The music drowns out voices, the noise of bottles, of tables,
of sudden movements, of falling bodies bloody at mouths,
noses, hands.
Feeling weak and discouraged, I say goodbye, to no purpose.
The voice keeps on telling me how it's made a habit, a way
of life of inaccuracy, in the hope of reaching accuracy from
the opposite direction.
A short blond man near us eavesdrops and laughs, looks
around, laughs and listens, his little eyes sparkling.
Alone now in the corner, a few unwonted tears on her face,
the broad-hipped girl carefully examines the edges of her
torn blouse.
Their backs turned and their shoulders compact, the three
customers watch the musicians, tap their feet to the rhythm,
smoke and clutch money in their hands.
A distant bell tolls over the music, the voices, the
generalized noise and the emptiness, over the echoless gulf
that separates the stranger's arms from
Persephone.
The girl with the hips gives a sigh unsuited to her
abundance. A customer strokes her thighs. The short man is
gone.
The stranger and Persephone amble off arm in arm, in
search of a bed; before disappearing beyond the doorway she
turns her head and looks at me.
So does he, but with a sly, triumphant air.
And the voice drones on about Achilles' shield, about the

Gray Sisters and the Hesperides, about golden apples and
water shining alike under the sun.
About Tarsis and Carthage, about the seven secret faces of
God, about the Virgin Mary and the world and the light.
About the need to write a book dealing with the Outer
Lands, even describing mountains, prostitutes and rivers,
since for a long time literature has only traveled through the
Inner Lands.
Persephone's dark traces persist, like a painful stain on the
doorway.
Moses continues to part the Red Sea, Orpheus urges on the
battered *Argo,* and a legendary, anonymous poet rouses
morning at midnight, makes the sun open its lids in the
middle of the moon.
I say goodbye to the brothel and the voice.
I step into the street and the chilly dawn, where the moon is
only the moon, without solar eyelids.
Passing by a mirror I glimpse my face, drunken and ugly.

A few days later I saw her again, sitting at a table with the
stranger. Her hands were fiddling with his. She looked at me
as if she'd been expecting me.
They were at the back of the big room, almost hidden by the
penumbra and the columns. It was obvious that they had
been drinking for some time. The stranger had the hiccups.
Persephone made a face, amused at seeing him and seeing me.
She stood up. Came toward me, with the gleeful air of
playing a joke on the man she was leaving. Smiled at me.
Took my face in her hands and forced me to look at her.
When the musicians began to play, she said we should
dance. I caught sight of the disconsolate stranger, still sitting
at the table, looking incredulous and somewhat abashed.

She pressed her breasts against my chest, as if she wanted to separate me by force from what I was seeing or might see. I felt her thighs probing me, her nails digging into my back. The stranger nervously drank glass after glass. He was the stealthy witness to whatever we were doing, to whatever we couldn't do in front of him.

To distract me from him, she began to talk about the need to see each other some other day, about her interest in me, about how I shouldn't let myself be misled by the interpretations her actions might suggest to me.

She kissed me surreptitiously on the lips, on my right cheek. At the end of the song she went smilingly to his side, without saying a word to me. Stroked his arms. Sat on his lap.

Soon afterwards they went off.

A week went by and I ran into her in the street. She was with him, laughing. They were swaggering along, their arms linked. The man was tall, almost out of proportion next to her.

They greeted me politely, invited me to go on with them to a nearby bar where jazz was played, where some, they said, smoked marijuana.

Persephone sat down next to me, talked on and on without paying much attention, because he was fondling her thighs or her breasts, or tickling her.

We drank avidly, without realizing how much wine we were drinking. From time to time Persephone would stretch her legs out over mine, to rest her feet. At times his hand was under her thighs and on top of my legs.

He carried it off naturally, feigned not to bear me a grudge, to be used to her liberties.

Until she suddenly took me by the hair, to pull me to her
lips and kiss me. And not for one second, or ten, but for
almost more than a minute.
That was when he opened his mouth immoderately wide,
without being able to say anything, sputtering in a kind of
snorting groan, like someone trying to talk, act and think all
at once.
That was when he said that the two of them should move to
another table to talk over the situation, to dot the *i*'s and
cross the *t*'s, because he didn't understand anything
anymore.
Because something funny was going on, and she wasn't the
same when she saw me, and he suspected, because of what
he'd seen so far, that his presence was going to become a
nuisance any minute now.
Needless to say, he had known her for some time, but it
wasn't easy to understand what she wanted, nor to say that
her way of settling things was cold-blooded and intransigent.
In short, he was a little afraid of her and kind of admired
her; she had often puzzled him, she had left him in doubt,
she had made him feel insignificant, small, burdensome.
But this afternoon he was not in the mood, or the mood had
been used up, or he no longer wanted to be in the mood to
put up with these stunts, and it should be understood once
and for all that she was the guilty one, she was the whore.
All this as if he was explaining it to me, while constantly
monitoring my reactions and hers, while repeatedly pointing
a threatening finger at her and at me.

They sat down next to me again, in an atmosphere of
troubling silence. Persephone's cheeks were red and her eyes
moist. He buried his head in his hands, staring intently at

the ashtray overflowing with butts. A waiter came up to ask
if he felt sick, "because the gentleman," he told us, "is a
regular customer," and he went away.
The man raised his face stupidly, like someone who has a
concussion without crying. He looked at her, he looked at
me. A lock of hair lay across his forehead, his ears were
sweaty. His flat stare wanted to intimidate us with its fixity.
He parted his lips, stammered at length in order to say, "I
can't talk." He put his hand into his inside jacket pocket,
showed Persephone a bunch of papers, cards, documents,
which she tore up, looking at me uneasily. He shrugged his
shoulders, shivering.
I threw the torn papers on the floor.

The man stood up, threw some money on the table to cover
the bill, brushed off his suit with his hand, looked at his
shoes and walked off with his head held high.
Two huge black women began to sing, swaying their hips,
rounding their mouths as if they were bleating. I remember
their red vests, their white pants.
Persephone touched my sex, slipping her hand through the
unzipped fly. All around us there was noise and penumbra,
plaintive voices, scumbled jumbled heads dancing.
Outside night had fallen. We were at the beginning of
something, in the nostalgia of an euphoria yet to come.
The next hours were already foreseen, were links in a chain
giving way, were little bodies of an unpredictable woman
falling one by one.
A thought, a vision had more weight than all the objects
picked up in a year. But we felt that poetry, which belongs
to no one, was yielding to us.
We told each other we preferred anger to weeping, silence to

shouting. We told each other that memories wouldn't be possible if time didn't move backward; that the wisest among men, the least subject to time, is he who remembers best. But that night I thought, for the first time without anguish, that I had never lost my past, and everyone else's, in such a satisfactory, definitive way.

We went into the street. There were clouds instead of stars and a moon. The street lamps lent an air of insubstantiality to the few hurrying passersby.
The bar and the customers jabbering inside it were left behind, like a diverse echo that dwindles and finally fades away as it breaks up.
The clouds covered part of the night; hanging low and enveloping, they were a living specter, massive and electric. It was hot and the buildings seemed tall, mute witnesses to the imminence of rain.
Persephone was laughing, and it was as if a diminutive moving space became populated all at once by white sounds and by thunderbolts crashing in the distance.
We heard a loud crack, a whiplash in the air, an acute pain, a tension being rent apart, that was hurtling downward over us.
Countless drops fell.
We saw the movement, the saturated darkness, the wet moment opening and closing behind each scurrying pedestrian, behind each door, window.
We saw the darkness resplendent in its watery collapse.

The desk clerk gave us a room, handed the keys to a young man, assured us there would be no interruptions, that we could feel at home.

The bellboy led the way in silence, looking sideways at
Persephone, especially at Persephone's breasts; he shifted
the key ring from one finger to another.

When we reached 124, he wished us good night, swallowing
his words, not really wishing us anything. He turned his
back to us, looking at her but not at me. We watched him
go away, before entering the room. He was clinking the
keys.

We locked the door. Stood still. Leaning against the wall, I
waited for her to express an attitude of mine.

She began to undress. Slowly and observing herself, as if
unfolding a reluctant nakedness that seemed to shrink into
itself.

Her round, white left thigh was arched.

She remained suspended for a few moments in the mirror.
She perused the inflections, the details of her body, of her
face. She was visibly gratified to look at herself and know
that I was looking at her.

She summoned me to the center of the room to embrace her,
to feel her presence physically. She laughed and cried
talking about something, remembering a story I listened to
without hearing.

She drew me to the bed, gave me little kisses while holding
me, sliding beneath me, removing my clothes amid tender
words.

She undid her hair. I felt her skin, her damp mouth, her
agile thighs. In her smoky aquarium I experienced a warm
spiral, another Persephone.

We were like a memory, like an incarnate purposeful
dream, like the window over there which is in harmony with
the doors and the walls and the other windows and the
air.

Outside the rain was the murmur, the light on our riverbed, drowsy and cradling embrace.

She was not wholly that public nakedness, those murky days with the brothel regulars, that cloudy afternoon in another town with touristy sunglasses and a drunken, flashy companion.
She wasn't that makeup-stained wall, nor the money that changed hands, nor the dirty, smelly sheet, nor the memory of that particular stranger.
That was only a disturbing anecdote.

I study the ceiling and the dead fire, the conflict of flesh that flesh resolves, Persephone's reserve as she comes out of the bathroom, her hands holding her robe closed, a drop of water on her cheek.
I hear the voice of a trinkets peddler, bawling threadbare promises that hoodwink solitude for a second.
I look at the absence of displaced beings, of displaced shadows. The musicians are drumming, an uninhibited whore shimmies naked on the stage, just like a snapshot.
The mill wheel goes round, even if it's invisible.

We eat side by side, without speaking. We look out the window.
Objects rise; in the dim light two black pupils rise.

Summer was beginning. The air was clear and life was fatal at each instant.
There was warmth in words, an overflowing landscape, a girl talking through Persephone's lips.
A group of youths went by. They wore circles of lights

around their waists, sexual serpents biting them above and below.
We lay down on the beach beneath the docile twinkling of the stars. A white bowl descended over my body.
But rivers have already passed where I am just arriving.

Let those who dare write of suffering, time has never had memory, only those who came back, but not time itself.
Beauty belongs to whoever can name it at the moment.
Everything alive is inevitable. Everything alive must brim over.
We are in the world, we know it, it's an open coffin always moving.

She looks over my shoulders, there it dawns, there day crosses with its burden of roots. There night falls.
Sounds come in from the street. Faces, messages and objects lost years ago.
A thunderbolt comes in that makes the afternoon shudder.
Time grows heavier and heavier.

Persephone only casts shadows, only repeats noises.
She looks at herself in the mirror three times. Looks about as if nobody was there.
Wonders what to wear. Ticks off colors to herself. Chooses yellow.
A yellow brassiere. Underpants. Yellow pantyhose.
Already everything seems given over to the nocturnal silence.
Her breasts in the brassiere are netted fish.
Standing by the bed she imprisons her legs.
She returns to the mirror, her mouth half open. Puts on a shift.

Powders her face. Puts on lipstick. Accentuates the nature of
her eyes. Modifies the arch of her eyebrows. Is spellbound
by her reflection. As if she were climbing up herself and
found her real face through disguise.
She combs and uncombs her hair. Combs it again. Strokes
her belly. Pats her loose hair. Sprinkles a few drops of
perfume on it.
When she looks at me, her face is decrepit.
She picks out a necklace, among many. Puts it on, examines
it in the mirror. Barely opening her mouth, she tells me
she'll be ready soon.
She checks her purse. All in order.
She hangs it over her arm.

The light bulb is a gray pear. Brief specks of light go out on
the window. A dark beam reaches under the door. The
staircase drops to the next floor.
The chess set stays put. The glasses, the table, the chairs,
the bookcase stay put. The man in the photograph stays put.

Now the world has a roof of clouds, Now the world is getting
older faster. The earth is wrinkled. It's a sheet made of mud.
A mountain is an old woman sitting down.
We move inside a soft, benign shell. Among old buildings
and windows and old windowpanes.
A door opens. Invites us to enter. A cloud turns golden. It's
a fiery zigzag. A bird's eye is a light that sees.
We walk along soundlessly. We are furtive shadows. A
slender shape comes toward us like a breath of air: the
apparition disappears upon turning the corner.
Blurry trees are floating, blurry houses, blurry women who
cross the street yawning.

Faintly uttered words reach us, as if through a
keyhole.
There's something personal in the last yellow gleams.
Life is pale, and its slopes are pale.
The mist smudges outlines.
Here and there: smoke.
Flashes.
A blue-clad schoolgirl runs by, she bends her head, she has
blond hair.
The sad-faced monkey looks out of the store window, slides
its paws over the glass.
A group of women move from shadows to street light, such
meager street light they are really moving to another
shadow.
A homosexual with an umbrella says hello.
A girl with a dog smiles at me.
A woman looks at me looking at her from behind my glasses
as at an insect, with a dress and a package, under a
microscope.
A few children are playing in a courtyard.
An old lady is scratching her head.
A fat man like a turtle advances with mincing steps.
Where a businessman has stopped to write down the name of
a popular product, a blind man stumbles, palpates the
businessman and jeers at his baldness.
A pregnant woman buttons up her blouse, yanks her skirt
down; her balloon remains intact, like a hard ball.
Men look at us and dogs look at us.
Rats chase each other in a ruined building; there's a rusty
bucket, its rope rotted and frayed.
There are yellow flowers in the grass, there's a dark green in
the trees like a D-major.

The twilight fades. Electric light shatters on the
windowpanes.
There's a door, a window to the left. There's a door two feet
lower to the right.
A dog runs by with a string of empty cans tied to his tail.
Another dog is digging holes in the ground.
There's less light.
On the corner a man is punching the air and talking to
himself. He wears a rope instead of a belt. His shoes are
tattered, his shirt is torn over his navel and he has a wart on
his nose.
I say hello as I pass him.
He takes out a knife from inside his jacket. With a furious
look he conceals it between his hands. Crosses himself. And
goes off limping, cursing aloud, threatening me with his fists.
Farther away, he waves his hands as if there was something
he didn't understand.
Phantoms come towards us talking, walking, jingling their
coins like prosperous shopkeepers; they materialize on all
sides, paunches overflowing, faces smiling.
Old walls smelling of dust loom up before us.
People from whom we expect nothing laugh at our side.
Restaurants and squalid hotels fall behind.
Taciturn clay figures, cotton faces, floury hands, vulnerable
dummies, men who are more silhouette, more reflection,
more death than present time pass by.
The houses seem to be sleeping, to carry on an ancient,
dusty conversation. We can smell mildew in their windows
and moss on their stones. They look straight ahead.
Occasionally their walls are shaken, there is a voice on their
roofs.
Plaster falling off a wall mimics a man's posturing.

The dried flowers stuck to the windows have human features.
There are eyes, there's a facial glossiness to Persephone's
skin, elbows and stomach that imperceptibly takes on our
form.
A strange discord rules over all. Something holds the world's
fruitfulness in suspense. Thoughts, feelings hold back at the
edge. Skull, heart, testicles are naked flesh.
Leaves, bodies, smiles cast shadows.
Things have a kind of false double.
Dried roots are flush with pavement and earth.
Memories that were dressed in green, on which crowds of
birds sang, are bare trunks, demolished walls.
At some windows, at some street corners, a man goes by.
Between windows and corners there are eyes watching us,
there are whispers of time that withers. There are idle
doings. There are fat ghosts like bad dreams.
The flashes of lightning weave a luminous net. They open up
the dark vault and the evening into rays. They pull clouds
apart, are horses of fire.
The moss is on the stone, the termite is in the wood, the
glare is deafening.
The water flowing away takes the household slops with it,
makes puddles, landscapes.
One veil covers another, one gesture, another gesture.
The instant of that boy running after his pregnant mother is
irreversible; so is the wild look of that girl dashing by.

A voice is singing in that house; it reaches the street thin
and defenseless, calls to mind other voices.
Some women walk along conversing, they carry baskets filled
with bread and food, they go past us telling how they
prepare meal after meal, day after day.

White wrinkles accompany their complaints.
There's a smell of earth, of dying plants on the balconies.
Timid girls lean over talking softly.
There's a smell under the earth, a penetrable hollow, a
cavity just for us.
There's a shoe full of holes, bodies that have mingled and
taken root in the earth.
There's a smell, a pain that walks beneath our feet, a
melancholy, someone bound and buried, a name that has
been lost.
In our memory the yellowish light bulb, our hands joined as
in a ritual go by.
A gray silence arises covering the almost dead, almost
devoured afternoon.
An indecision of rain hovers over our own indecision, over
our women and our shadows.
This dry clap of thunder crashing down like the groaning
peal of a bell is impossible.

The clouds seem like heavy, dirty hours, high clouds of ebony.
They hold waters that don't flow. They are sponges of gloom,
rolling blackness, noisy heaps.
Beneath them birds flee from their disturbing omens.

The light is gray, and the passerby's face, and the unending
tension, and the anxiety of the man who keeps looking
upward as if expecting a cave-in although all he hears is the
absence of rain, the absence of those days when the charged
atmosphere finally begets thunder.

There is the sky, that was radiant at daybreak, now somber
above the houses.

There is the dust, covering mirrors and the tops of walls.
There are things, so entrenched in themselves it's impossible
not to fear them, not to regard them as specters.
There is the lightning, in a burning zigzag, as if something
very private were loudly splitting open.

We cross to the other side of the street. The whores are now
walking by our side; they cross the street with us.
The hour strikes on a short man's wristwatch, it also strikes
in the heart of the woman walking with him.
We reach the avenue. It branches into streets and alleys
where couples hang around, fornicate outdoors.
I look at Persephone's shadowed profile, the streetlight on
the pavement.
Black veils settle over trees and houses.

Night falls over the city.
Over the man staring at us, over the cars and my hands, and
over the cane of the old man who leans against a wall
coughing.
It surrounds Persephone's eyes, legs, shoes.
It takes over the tall and slender buildings.
Darkens my arms, my smile.

The dry shadows descend.
Night secretes opinions and footsteps.
Faces conversing beneath lampposts.
Prostitutes. Reporters. Storekeepers. Politicians.
They jostle each other in the street, try to disappear into a
movie theatre, look for the address where, they have been
told, a church has been built.

·   ·   ·

The brothel reappears as a place of copulation, of fantasy, of
postponement.
Persephone fastens her eyes on the bouncer's eyes, on the
first step.
Hate, love, clay, light only last a moment.

The hour slithers beneath the ceiling, lazy and red,
smokily evanescent. Heavy with penumbra, it reclines on
the air. Grows in a spiral, gravitates, strikes.
Wriggles like a worm, but invisibly.
Flies like a bird, but invisibly.
Passes like a man, but invisibly.
Pauses on our hands, and moves on. Pauses on mold, and
moves on. Wavers between our eyes, and moves on.
Lying on the ground, it continues.

The hour flows between word and gesture.
The hour is heard between silence and gesture.
Its progress makes the planks of the stage audible, makes a
nail scraped on skin audible.
Makes the pavement, the earth audible.
It meets questions, opinions, stockings, breasts,
sideways-looks head-on.
It doesn't cast a shadow, it does sow silences in the
midst of pandemonium, drown glasses, plates, mouths,
trousers.
It fell from darkness and reigns in darkness, like bees in the
dark.
It arrived with noise and revels in noise, like a wind
instrument.
Soon it will depart, impersonal and peopled, leaving traces

on the bodies it has grazed, branding everything that has no
soul.

The penumbra hides or distances faces, winks, shoes;
lengthens a nose, erases a mouth.
Shortens fingers, shelters an arm.
Makes a head grow.
Builds a pile of shadows. Cancels out solitary and mute
existences.
It is there, solid as a roof, a wall, a floor, as a secret,
maternal belly.

A reddish light tinges men and women alike with distance
and solemn comicality.
Smoke coming from all sides of the big room congeals into
an artificial cloud, a spreading mushroom.
A body extending its arms and legs seems to dismember
itself and point in four directions.
An old man's voice, louder than the others, falls silent when
I crush my cigarette on the floor.
Susi and Marta strut like sluggish, obscene pigeons. Their
bodies are impregnated with the smells of copulation. Sighs
of lust sigh in their flesh.
Wrinkles twitch on their faces. Pale nipples nestle at their
necklines.
Watery eyes look at me as if I didn't exist.
Their shadow creeps lengthily behind them.

Coins, paper and bills sodden with wine and ashes,
overturned bottles pointing their bottoms at the owner are
revealed by a busboy's flashlight.
Garish dresses and snazzy suits buzz like large colorful

insects. Cigarettes, pipes, cigars burn, stink in my face,
behind me, on my fingers: the half-light surrounding them
grows darker, becomes viscous.

A phonograph plays an endless song about desire and kisses,
a voice that stretches, shrinks, thins out and grows, until it
explodes into a rain of mingled instrumental sounds.

Tapping his pipe against his nose, the owner speaks to a
waiter seated on his right; the latter listens, his jaws
creaking in a yawn.

In the owner's speech the calm of a bored old man who'd
rather be alone so he can sleep is apparent; teeth clacking
together and hissing words are audible.

The waiter splays his hands wide inside his jacket pockets.
The faithful are there in their party clothes and party faces.
They talk listlessly, as if not expecting to be heard, or as if
they were of no interest to their partners; they leave
sentences half-finished, questions unanswered, continually
change the subject, repeat the same thing to two people,
stand up, cough, notice who's coming, who's leaving, who
isn't sitting with them at their table.

They applaud for no reason at all. Laugh for no reason at
all. Uncork a bottle. One of them says he hasn't slept all
night, another says he slept for three hours, another, that he
likes Marta, another, that his mother's sick.

I take a chess set out of my pocket. I take out a sprightly
knight, a bishop whose only remnants of episcopacy and
madness are the memory and the tonsure, a svelte, frigid
queen, a featureless king, castles, pawns.

I put a coin in the ashtray and stub out my cigarette on it. I
lay my arm over my heart: both are throbbing. I take off my
glasses. Loosen my tie, my belt. I look at Persephone.

We are alone but not alone. The drunks, the whores, the
zombies, the walls and the night accompany us in our
solitude. The chess set, its pieces lined up and ready to
begin the game, accompanies us with twenty possible plays
for each side.
I move the king's pawn to his fourth square.

Persephone is drinking next to me, pale and red. She drinks,
her eyes big and breasts enormous. She puts her feet on my
lap. She stares hard at me, the glass a translucent beard on
her chin, like a pharaoh.
Two or three couples are murmuring, hidden in the shadows.
They caress each other with dark arms. They open their
mouths just enough to knot their tongues, to brush their lips.
With trembling hands they travel over each other, lift the
dress up, unbutton the shirt. They lean against the wall,
slide down to the floor. They scramble and clamber and kiss.
They smell of sweat and saliva. Love glitters in their eyes.

A hunchback, too aware of his hump, comes in. Peers lewdly
at Susi, at Marta. Rivets his eyes on their thighs, breasts,
buttocks. Waves his arms about like an insect bothered by
its wings at the instant of flight. Takes a child's step.
Straightens his tie. Sneezes, stumbles from the jolt. But he
doesn't fall, and inches his way to a table.
Magdalena and Carmen come in, taking off their coats. M.
zips up her skirt, lifts it slightly to smooth her stockings, ties
a shoelace and sticks out her behind like an ostrich with its
head in the ground. C. laughs at nothing, laughs because she
is laughing, laughs at her laughter. When M. straightens up,
they quickly head for the checkroom.
An old man with a peg leg crosses the room after them,

walking like a woman in high heels. He wears a
short-sleeved striped shirt and he clenches and unclenches
his hands. He stops to light up a cigarette; his hip juts out
above his waist.

Pregnant Mariana arrives, in a tight dress with a design of
green flowers against a white background; she lumbers by,
swinging her fat arms and thin legs. Her fluffy gray hair falls
over her bare back. She halts at my table and looks at me
with a placental face.

Rosa, Rosaura and Rosamunda arrive, and Blanca, her
aggressive finger pointing at the peg-legged old man.

Carla, Lili and Jazmín arrive.

Rosaura and Blanca bow before the owner. Go to the
checkroom. Leave their coats. Lean against their respective
columns waiting to be called. Blanca, her face beaming,
makes an obscene gesture with her hand at Persephone.
Persephone returns it smiling.

Their arms linked, as if each was the other's woman, Carla
and Rosa stride across the room.

Carla tugs at her narrow skirt, her belt, her blouse. Her
rough movements are like an athlete's or a muscular
peasant's. She steps firmly and with the whole foot. Her
hostile face seems ready for any challenge. Seen head-on
she's flatter than any man.

Together they cross the threshold of copulation's dwelling.

Jazmín and Rosamunda's blue and black sweaters are too
tight, making their breasts more expressive than their faces,
masking their flaccidity, giving them an apparent consistency.
They throw their arms back to make their bosoms jut out.

Their flesh-colored stockings are more provocative than they themselves. They chat standing next to a column.
Three young men look them over. Make inaudible remarks about them.
Each holds a cigarette, and one of them coughs, as they approach the women.
Stop short before reaching them. Examine them.
The coughing one touches Rosamunda's shoulders, navel, a breast. Waits for her reaction . . . then grabs her.

The phonograph finishes one song. Begins another.
The crowd gesticulates dumbly, its voice annulled by the sound.
An excited rhythm is all that's heard.
The floozie comes in.
She hesitates at the door.
Looks at several faces.
Smiles to herself.
Opens her coat.
Her scanty breasts tremble, far apart.
She's naked from the waist up.
From waist to neck she looks bloodied in the red penumbra.
The owner applauds from the back of the room.
The customers laugh and applaud.
Mixed in with the music is the thumping of the peg leg.

People keep on coming in.
The braggart joins the dance; the aging man, taken unawares in the bathroom, joins the dance.
Two identical young men who might be twins enter, blend in; a pointy-fingered old man shaking his hands in the air, a sharp-chinned waiter enter, blend in.

Ana hangs on Lucrecia's right arm, a pretty-boy on her left.
Jazmín, Lili and Magdalena stand next to their columns like
three imperturbable, pop-eyed frogs.
Norma and Rosamunda dance together. Maria sticks close to
the wall.
An older woman flutters her handkerchief over two
inquisitive boys who are watching her; a fine dust floats in
the air.
"I'm so blind," she says, "that I can barely hear you."
When she closes her eyes, they notice that she has no
eyebrows or eyelashes.
Her lips curve like a membrane.
She lets go of the handkerchief in midair, as if seized by a
sudden pain.

The musicians, in their places, begin the night with a tango.
A group of young men by the window sing along.
The old man keeps the beat with his peg leg.
The hour enters striking nine times.
I see obscene drawings, mustaches, chins and noses,
perfumed, virile mustaches, round, hairless chins, small,
prying, obtuse eyes, faces in which one eye looks west and
the other east, flaring and pinched nostrils pointing upwards,
downwards; hairdos, mufflers, shawls, hands, knees and
heels; breasts like balloons that can pop out of brassieres
and float to the ceiling or drift into the street; hereditary
moles and painted moles, watermelon heads, huge naked
bellies like scaleless white fish about to give birth,
black-eyed masks, wigs, faces shaped like brains, hearts,
livers. The night is gravid with laughter and breasts, with
dresses and stockings, with words and chairs, with songs and
embraces.

The moonlight penetrates the window as if it were an
eggshell.
The musicians go on playing. Their sounds reverberate in
the dark brothel.
An ice cube melts on the floor. Bathes in itself while
melting.
A plate is broken. A chair grates. The image of love
dissolves.
Sows, vixens, bitches, monkeys, mares and she-asses gabble.
Susi and Maria go by. Berta and Angelica. Carmen and
Blanca. Burning cigarettes and voluminous trousers go by.
Outside the wind jeers, hurls swift bats like small whining
phantoms against the windows.
The world turns into another world.

Persephone drinks. She sweetens my lips with her wine.
Kisses me with lips, an icy tongue. Leaves ice cubes melting
in my mouth. Takes my face in her hands and lifts it up so
that I look into her eyes. They are moist, tearful.
I feel like laughing, so I take a drink. Right in the middle
of her serious scrutiny of something inside me.
I can't feel her.
She is talking to me, but I'm so close to laughter that I can't
hear her words, to a laughter that blots her out, that wants
to turn towards darkness and laugh alone.
So I clench my teeth and put on a look of false concern
and say two or three rhetorical things about love. And to
squelch my laughter I recite a few lines by a classical poet
about life.
She listens to me. And holds my head against her chest. And
kisses my hair and my hands. And wets my right cheek with
her tears.

And I smile with my eyes, my lips and my soul. And she
smiles, looking at me. And I tell her that I'm laughing from
joy, that we hadn't been so close for a long time.
Her presence seems to recede into memory, to be less real
than the pack of cigarettes I fiddle with; she seems to go
out, to disappear into the penumbra.
I see nothing where she sits. Her movements are smoke. Her
hands holding my face are the hands of a drunken fool.
She kisses me, smiles at me, assures me that our next
embrace will be more intense and prolonged than ever.
But I don't feel any desire for it, I can't picture what she's
promising.
Only a swarm of bees and prostitutes surrounds me, buzzes
at me, whispers to me.
There are scratches and wrinkles on the tables and on her
fingers, on the walls and on her breasts, on her forehead, on
her stomach, on her hips, next to her eyes, on her elbows
and knees.
Death and forgetting are at work on the gaiety and sleekness
of her face.

The wary customers who have impaled a host of sexes on a
single sex are already here, the men who have climbed the
entrance stairs nonchalantly, as if obeying a habit, an
involuntary desire: they are slow to think and express
themselves.
We are already here, ensconced in our places, taking up
space, a chair, an attitude for the night;
already taking up the next words, the next fond expression
that will appear on our faces as if against our will.
The storekeeper, the whore, the thief and the poet are
already here, already sleeping under the same roof.

Susi gets down on all fours and walks like a dog. She bares
her teeth, her gums, swallows her saliva. Barks ferociously.
She smells the floor, sniffs the air as if following a trail.
She scratches her armpits and her head. Lifts her left leg as
if to urinate.
She waggles her behind at me, at the owner.
She barks her way to a young man. Puts her finger on his
fly. Takes the glass out of his hand and drinks.
She stands up wearily and walks away on unsteady legs.
Disappears among the others.

A hand emerges from beneath a table and turns off a red
light.
It goes under again.
Four legs joined in a kind of struggle emerge confusedly.
Persephone dances with the owner. She slumbers in herself,
like someone who doesn't know in whose bed she's fallen.
She hums the song.
One of her eyes is hidden behind the owner.
She flows smoothly along the rhythm she hears, in the midst
of the smoke.
Other couples dance near them.
Slow and self-conscious, thin and fat, they blot out, reveal
Persephone and the owner.
They glide with the sound, patiently, hastily.
They make the penumbra denser, the diameter of the stage
narrower.
Some of them yawn parenthetically while performing the
steps the music dictates or clasping their apathetic partners
more tightly.
Sonia looks out of Persephone's eyes. Susi and Maria look
out. Rosa and my own eyes look out.

The musicians are drumming, breaking the continuity of the tune to which they had accustomed us.

She dances, nimble in each step she adds to the previous one, as if only the owner existed for her.

From the way they hold each other and move, both seem to have been drawn to the other for a long time.

People keep on arriving.

Shirts, heads and shoes jostle each other at the entrance.

Words, shouts and curious looks intermingle.

The girl with broad hips allows herself to be led, without a glance for the man who presses her to his chest, as if she was about to break away from him at any moment.

Magdalena dances with her back to the customer who hugs her, her hips swiveling almost angrily against the fire of masculinity.

The floozie, her breasts bared, approaches the new arrivals, welcomes them, asks two or three to dance, is rebuffed by all.

A tall fat man agrees to dance with the little prostitute; he takes her by the arm, leads her to where the others are dancing.

With difficulty she holds on to his shoulders, hangs on him, pushing and curving herself against his stomach, beneath a sudden outpouring of sounds.

People keep on arriving.

Clara and Esponja come in, Guadalupe, Pilar, Lourdes, Fátima, Consuelo and Socorro, and three more women, known as the Celestial Trinity.

Ignacio, Francisco and Agustín, Santiago and Tomás, José, Felipe and Genovevo.

A monk disguised as a businessman and an eccentric
professor with a bushy mustache, who dreams of athletes and
has written a book about supermen, arrive; a youth who
smiles, there in the doorway; a blue-eyed girl whose name is
Carolina; another Maria, whom we call the Egyptian, to tell
her apart from the first one.
The owner kisses Persephone on the neck. She giggles.
Their shadows beneath the red bulbs are four long shadows.
But I only see one body. One back. One hand.
Two bodies in profile that aren't theirs.
Viviana puts her hands into the inside pockets of a
white-haired man's jacket, just like in a movie. She
unbuttons his shirt and steals while he sleeps on with his
eyes open watching her.
Magdalena tells two customers who are near me how she got
her start in promiscuous love.

The musicians stop playing. Catch their breath. Exchange a
few quick words among themselves. Sit down.
Now voices, hiccups, falling objects, footsteps, chairs and
tables being moved can be heard.
The room smells of sex, liquor and cigarettes.

Jazmín tries to hide from a waiter who's following her. She
crouches behind a column. Sticks her head out. The waiter
sees her.
Susi shouts out the name of someone who hesitates to cross
the threshold. The young man or old man stands motionless,
not hearing his name, not picking out the word that
designates him as the object of the clamor.
The musicians' bodies come to life again. The instruments
take up the beat.

Young and middle-aged prostitutes, notorious or obscure,
covered up or half-naked, stand up to dance.
Two men simultaneously hold out their hands to the same
available girl who, like an automaton, chooses one of them,
takes his arm and goes off with him.
Persephone's and the owner's heads protrude above the
other heads. Cheek to cheek, they form a two-faced body.
They keep rubbing against each other, brushing their thighs
together, sweating at the temples.
Persephone's expression is vague, her chin is propped on the
owner's shoulder as if her head had separated from the rest
of her body and was only a face, a vagueness with no trunk.

Katy and Susana, Beatriz and Rosalinda, Cunina, Edulia and
Putina, Liliana, Milly and Francisca arrive. Paola stands in
the doorway, she doesn't leave but she isn't here.
There are smells left, right and center.
There are eyes and ears watching and listening at the tables,
behind the columns, in the hallway, in the bathrooms.
Greed, ambition, egotism, need glitter on some faces like
physical features, like virtues or defects, like a freckle under
the ear, like a snub nose or cross-eyes.
The instants elapse, blowsy and thick, hefted by alcohol, by
penumbra.
A girl walks towards a young man, her arms outstretched,
her pastel dress round as a bell. That customer disappears,
but he won't be the last: still others enter, mix with the men
talking near the entrance.
I see light-green bottles, a doll run through by a knife on
that chair.
I hear the women who pray while they drink, who speak as
if chanting litanies.

. . .

The floozie examines a portrait missing an eye, runs her
finger over the faded beard, the white chin.
She takes a pair of scissors from her bag and cuts out
something which becomes a bird.
When she's done, she puts it on the table, opens her bag
again.
She places two rolls on a napkin, one stale and one fresh,
half a cold roast chicken, and a jar of fruit cocktail.
She puts her hand into her coat sleeve and draws out a bill,
reads the amount and puts it away quickly, looking around
to make sure no one has seen her.
Spreads her breasts apart as if she were brushing hair off
her chest. Begins to eat, her eyes hungry.
She offers a bite to a nonexistent friend, to a phantom guest
who doesn't even have a chair.
She spills water on the table. Simpers at those who stare at
her coldly or in disgust.
While she eats she gathers up what is inedible, carefully
arranges it again in her purse and takes out a hand
mirror.
She laughs at her reflection and makes a face.
Still eating, she puts the mirror down, but the fixed grimace
remains.
She talks to herself rapidly, gesticulating.
Her face is covered with freckles, her fingernails dirty and
her hair stringy.
She smells of newborn baby and corned beef.
She chews. Blows her nose. Brings her hand to her eyes and
peeks between the fingers.
A misplaced dream speaks in her eyes. She takes her hand
away from her face and plays with some coins.

She bends over the table. Turns her back to me. Tells
herself she feels lonely, that she has a calling for suffering,
that she would regret not suffering.
She chews on her words when she speaks. Scratches her
head, an arm, a knee.
Grimaces and hiccups.
She huddles in the chair like an ailing bird.
She sings so sadly and faintly that she's scarcely heard.
Shakes her purse to muffle the sound of her singing.
An old man next to her begins muttering a steady *iiiiii*, as
if he were a saw.

With feathers hanging in her face and a flower in her mouth,
Susi leans on her elbows, head in hands.
A boy who gives off a dirty, rustic smell touches her.
Squeezes the cups which restrain her breasts. Explores the
tight edge of her neckline. He pulls her dress down, his
hands lingering over her thighs.
She hears him talking too fast to be understood, making
gestures to back himself up that are transfixed in midair
when he can't go on with what he's saying.
And in the end she lets him grasp her wrists and force her
to kneel.
He reconnoiters her, smells her, prowls around her body.
She uncovers a breast, asks him to bend over, sticks it in his
mouth.
He fondles her with long, hairy fingers.
She, kneeling, looks at him tenderly. Whispers to him, and
murmuring into his ear, bites it. He tries to clasp her, but
she repulses him, her eyes shut tight.
He wants to leave, but she holds him back, kisses him, bares
her other breast, sneezes.

He circles her kneeling body. Rubs his fingers over her face,
thighs and breasts.
She bends her head to see what he sees.
He slaps her weakly.
She stands up and embraces him. They are a two-headed
animal.
They whisper together. Bend over simultaneously. Fall to the
ground.
They wallow, they thrash, they labor on the floor.

There is panting which doesn't come from them. There's a
noise of voices and steps hemming them in.
There's a hubbub, a confusion of ears and feathers.
Everywhere there are noses and eyeballs. Male and female
genitalia.
They will only shut their eyes to sleep or die.
They can breathe in the brothel, here they are realities.
They are here as if by sleight of hand.
They issue from the walls, the hallway, the bathrooms.
They take root in a hollow, in a corner, in any sex; they
germinate everywhere, come from everywhere.
They fall upon the women, upon themselves, upon the
chairs.
They look and listen, they're on the stage, in the doorways,
in the space that separates one table from another.
Their noses are pressed to the panes, their eyes glued to the
print in a newspaper, to the advertisements plastered here,
there.
Anxious for a certain something, worn out by that certain
something. Always standing up straight, always growing.
Run aground on a sentence they've been repeating for years,
bringing it out every minute as a sudden revelation.

Stuck in a moment, in a memory, not wanting to go ahead,
not wanting to leave.

Multiplying themselves, leaving residues and traces of their
crumbling time that comes and goes like a moan.

Comparing recent pictures with old ones, with the intent
faces of their predecessors.

Doubting which way to go, towards where earthworms
gestate to perish, towards where objects repose in an
inorganic sleep.

While there is something in the curtains, the footsteps and
the questions that goes that has gone forever.

And there's a smell of dust, a sense of oblivion on the floor
and on the walls.

Everything falls forever, everything happens and falls,
revolves, falls.

The spiraling hour touches the ceiling like a curl of smoke,
the seconds whir in the air. Some set their watches ahead or
back, mistaking the hour that strikes godlike in the distance.

Young men toy erotically with young women.

Elderly men fan the embers in elderly women's bellies; they
mutually consume their final ardors.

The braggart drinks out of four bottles in a row. He speaks
in a throaty voice to Blanca (who watches him as she dances
with a shadow) and shows her a jar in which captive flies,
spiders and cockroaches fight and devour each other.

Leaning against a column, the owner smokes, fondles his
pipe with his fingers. Half closing one eye, he seems to be
taking in Susi's dress, cleavage, stockings, buttons, shoes.
He signals her to throw back her shoulders more, to
straighten up.

She obeys.

Persephone goes to the checkroom or the bathroom.

. . .

A man with a broken nose goes by. Katy and Maria go by.
The old man goes by who invaded his daughter's bed,
awakening the young girl's body until she desired no other
breaching, no other grief than what he gave her at night.
But who is this who claims all Alma's loving for himself,
when the most that can be expected of her is the love she
never had; solemn and bald, he says words to her too
passionate to be credible.
The darkness increases, the shadows elbow each other.
In the densest parts, only cigarette smoke reveals that people
are there.
Other voices join my voice, speak at the same time as mine
does.
I turn my head. I look. Magdalena is smiling behind me.
Her eyes concentrate on something which she alone sees.
Her lips part. She doesn't move an eyelash, noise, movement
don't move her.
I blow into Persephone's hand mirror: I see myself blurred
through the blurred vapor. I wipe myself off with another
breath and my forearm.
Faces I had never seen appear, words I had not heard
before.
Many images seethe at once, many ways of walking, of
dancing, of seizing and rejecting.
Foolish questions, insoluble questions are raised. Beings one
could love do not achieve existence.
Pristine thoughts occur to me, crowd each other, become
muddled, and trying to express only one makes me stammer.
But permanence stands up to illusion, the day confronts
anguish, deep in the night the first seed of light germinates.
Against all unreality there is God.

Although while we dream, sometimes and now, the reality of
the dream we are dreaming awakens us, and dawn is heard
farther off in our desire than something dreamed a thousand
years ago.

There is a sudden hush. The owner points to a dark corner.
Dissimilar voices draw attention to a dark corner. The
shadows are thickest there where they point.
A circle of green and blue light opens in the center, a pencil
of light drives off the darkness, illuminates a single body,
colors a single body.
The penumbra is snuffed out in the room.
Clients and whores in a circle expectantly observe what is
moving inside a yellow dress.
Sound after sound falls, movement after movement.
Persephone stands out among the women who surround her,
as if phosphorescent. Her dress gives off smoke.
Her eyes closed, she throws a mirror on the floor.
She has her hands on her hips. She chews on the stem of a
flower. She struts, holding up one finger in the air.
She's like a wild beast, grown old and hairy.
She puts her hands to her eyelids for a moment, and opens
them. Puts her hands on her head, makes horns.
Her eyelids turn blue, her eyes glitter.
She lifts her dress, shrugs off the shoulder straps. Wiggles
her hips. Mumbles or ruminates some words through closed
lips.
She eats with her stare, drinks with her pupils. Her eyes
pause at a corner of the ceiling.
She hears the noise of a glass breaking, the silence of the
broken glass. The floorboards creak beneath her feet.
It is Susi who twists in her belly, Magdalena in her thighs, it

is she and it isn't she who is dancing, but it is she and all
the others.
She flings away rings, necklace, shoes, pretends she's
receiving very heavy objects in exchange.
She has a belt in one hand, and her navel is slightly sunken.
Her lips are so thin they look like two blades.
She barely leans on her right heel, barely touches the floor.
A kind of gladness shines in her face.
She mutters to herself, gives the impression of dictating what
her next move should be.
She prods her flesh with a fingertip, avidly submerges it into
her round stomach.
Her body casts two shadows on the floor.
She throws her opened hands back over her shoulders, as if
she were scattering pebbles or human gems behind her.
We can hear her panting.
She makes believe someone is pursuing her: the pencil of
light pursues her.
She makes believe someone catches up with her, bites her
breasts, her thighs and her lips.
She feigns going off with him, taking leave of everyone.
But she stops at the doorway which leads to copulation's
dwelling.

The night also rages, the minute rages. The eyes watching
her, the window. Night burns up in the purple radiance. A
secret confusion settles into my voice. A cascade of sound
makes me old, pains me.
Everything is fictitious. It's all a pretext, a way of
pretending, of having fun. She is dancing for the sake of
dancing, to stretch her legs, to keep from being bored, to
keep darkness from devouring her.

Such is her way of singing: making haste; such is her way of
being mine: not being mine.
The spotlights play over her shoulders, crisscross her face,
weave shadows in her hair, on her stomach, on her knees.
They follow her to a column, to a table, touch only one
thigh, the shape of her foot, the leg of a chair, the face of a
spectator.
She opens her hands and separates the fingers. With long
silent glances she studies each body, each face. Speaks in a
low yearning voice. Covers her ears, closes her eyes, takes a
step.
She seems to be seized by sudden shudders of happiness and
dread.

She spreads her thighs, throws herself to the floor, falls on
her knees, as if her entire being were drawn downwards.
One hand is on her stomach, the other is clenched in the air.
She rubs her breasts, her hips; her shoulders tremble; she
tucks in her chin toward the base of her neck.
She remains motionless, her mouth agape, as if
dumbfounded, as if in ecstasy, as if life had abandoned her,
like a part of myself there at the center.

They sprinkle the oval drums with rum, gin and whiskey.
A woman who's watching plays with three rings. She slips
them on and off her fingers.
Frail young girls laugh as virile objects are thrust into them.
The musicians sing in languishing voices, spread their song
with a whine.
A young drunk says to his alleged friend,
"Roldán, you should give her a try."

.   .   .

Persephone lies down, puts her ear to the ground, listening
to whatever walks in the distance or whatever is heard
below.

She writhes forward, using her elbows for support and
propulsion, her hands open flat as if she were delivering an
offering.

Her breasts hang down, her round, white behind is blue. Her
belly grazes the floor voluptuously, albeit slackly.

She moves her lips.

She stands up, suddenly filled with impatience.

She bends over, touches the floor with her fingertips without
flexing her knees, as if doing exercise.

Her face seems to be made of green blood, black furrows
and deep wrinkles.

She waves her underwear in the air.

The spotlights leave her in the shadows. The drums can still
be heard, as if the celebration were continuing in the dark.

She centers herself again beneath the pencil of light, takes
up her body in motion, looks at the stares dangling from
her.

The musicians encourage her, lead her on, improvise.

She's drenched with sweat, panting. Disheveled, naked,
unapproachable.

When she raises her arms, her makeup runs, slides down
her face.

Her nose lengthens, becomes crooked, hangs over her parted
lips.

Her eyebrows, her eyelashes are blue. Her eyes chestnut
green. Her lips black and narrow.

Her chin quivers like an old lady's. Her splayed fingers are
rigid.

She seems to be standing a few inches above the floor.
The spotlights and the makeup turn her cheeks green, then
blue.

The smoke rises, forms a constellation on the ceiling.
New heads, peering over each other, have made the air
warmer.
Persephone's navel stares out like a rough cut at the
beginning, like a gesture of her abdomen.
Her flowing hair gleams more naked than her body, the
sharp chin poised on her right shoulder is more naked than
her body.
Imperceptibly, her eyes become gray again, her brows
delicate and black, her lips red.
She brushes her hand over her gyrating sex.

The musicians take a break.
Shouts and word are born.
Persephone stands unmoving, her thighs parted.
The owner watches. Maria watches. The waiters watch. A
thirteen-year-old girl, damp and trembling, watches.

Some of the customers study her like stern judges, their
faces propped on their hands.

The drums break into the intermission. The sobriety of a
piano sounds remote.
Sounds of skin and wood mingle with remarks. The whores
let themselves be touched by hidden hands: heavily
breathing men grope at them from behind like anxious,
blindfolded beggars.

The youngest among them cover their breasts with their
arms when I turn around and look at them.
Persephone disappears into the darkness. The blue breast.
The pink thighs.
She reappears beneath the tenuous reddened light. Rolls her
round belly. Opens her hands.
She heads for the stage, where the musicians are whinnying.
She feigns a hot pursuit, an ample repentance.
Fastens her eyes on her toes.
From far off she has an archaic face.

She dances on the past, not on the present. She dances to
attain quietude. She wraps her bleak future in the music.
Eyes sprout on the door. On Susi's chin, on my hands.
Squinting and hidden they focus on her, they touch her
movement, her emptiness, her abundance.
They revolve around her waist, her neck, her legs. They
come and go on her belly, her arms, her hair as if in a club
where they can lie down, daydream, walk about and sleep.

The musicians, whose cheeks are swollen, faces elongated
and mouths like zeros, lean slightly to the right.
Two of them are singing, another follows like an echo.
A young prostitute smiles at me.
And I am like someone alien and speechless, who doesn't
fully understand what's going on around him, what's
happening to him, what pretense he should invent for the
others when he awakens upon being observed.
Then suddenly and making an effort he feels that he has a
face, he emerges from the dream he was dreaming,
and he doesn't know what to say, what to do, how to take
shape before those who are watching, surprised unawares

and far from the moment, far from what's going on right
next to him, from what's happening to him, too hazy to
explain himself, seeing everything all of a sudden, hearing
everything, losing what had gone forever, losing what is
occurring now.

Even though a fat man whispers to me between hiccups that
the prostitute is a young man wearing makeup who arrives
in a different disguise every night, docile and tender.
And because he seems to be the most beautiful of all the
whores, many have only realized the imposture in his arms,
and have slapped him, partly because he wasn't what they
saw, partly because of the perseverance of his excess, since
some of them have taken him to bed several times, beguiled
by the unexpectedness of the disguise, or by the novel way
of alluring them.
Whether man or woman, he disappears among the others, no
more is left of him than a cigarette butt on the floor and the
customer's eyes searching with fervor and malice.
Other feet stand in the space he filled before, other faces are
in the place where his face smiled, from where he left on
account of a few words.
Tomorrow she will be another, a new disguise and a new
body; she will pass by me without future or past, alone and
unrecognized, but somehow still part of yesterday, in her
amended and sterile expression.

Persephone beneath the pencil of light examines her navel as
if her existence were drawn inwards through that indentation.
She slowly contracts her body, lifts one foot slightly. White
fingers of her hand waving in the darkness. White teeth seen
from below.

She squats as if on a bench flush with the floor.
Jiggles her knees together.
She rocks her behind. Opens and closes her thighs,
concentrating on doing it, as if she only lived in that act, at
that instant.
Her eyes look all around her body, as if trying to escape
from a cage.
She lies down facing the ceiling. Breathes in gasps. She
sways her procreative tomb, with difficulty raises it a few
inches.
She opens her mouth, gives the impression, by her groans,
that she is about to expel a demon or a toad. But she covers
her face with her hands. Throws her head backwards,
concealing her expression.
She spreads her thighs wide apart. Her sex stares out, labial,
open. Her hesitation, her suspense foretell an event, a yes, a
no, a complete overflowing.
When a pale dampness comes over her, a quivering in the
cheeks, a letting go, a sundering, a final and applauded
ecstasy.

The music stops, although the last note seems to tarry, to
fade away in its immobility.
We feel the heat, the lack of a place to put our hands, the
need not to look at where she still is.
Silence asserts itself among the voices like a void within my
own body, like a private place to which I withdraw.
I'm looking, but not at the bald man's baldness nor Susana's
red dress. I hear only one voice, clear and fluid, but I don't
understand.
I submerge myself outside, I bare all to the exterior, my
heart striking full of noise.

I stifle something within me that tells me what I am not.
I think I sleep a moment, draped over the table I've been
looking at, over the glass with dregs of wine, among
cigarette butts.
I think I applaud, upon awakening, my own, my brief
inexistence.
I count mustaches retreating from the battlefield, pallid and
red noses.
Others' feelings, stupid remarks, insidious longings to be
deaf.
Eyes that only convey coldness, coldness, coldness.
Bodies that pile up and give off smoke. Lines on the wall
that run straight, curve and are truncated.
Hands, which are mine, thrust in pockets.

Everything passes, but part of what passes remains, halts in
its flight.
Everything disappears into itself. Everything needs an hour
its own size to disappear.

I see Susi.
I see your sex, Persephone.
I see the bald man.
I can no longer hide, I can't stop seeing myself amidst the
prostitutes and the chairs.
The little whore, the hoodlum with the cocked eyebrow will
be with me forever.
I will be here again, on the fringe of the party, telling
myself it doesn't exist, that the party didn't exist, only those
who want to, those who wanted to celebrate, and those who
will turn or have turned all this into the insubstantial stuff of
memory.

I remain in the penumbra like an actor with no place on the stage, who whispers, yawns and shivers without anyone noticing him; unremarked by the audience and the other actors, who refuse to see him, soliloquizing and repeating old-fashioned phrases, with a stiff expression and an annoying, inconsequential melancholy that slowly abandons him, leaving him all alone.

Without any merits to show off, because he distrusts merit; without anything to say to the others or to himself, since whatever he could say is happening too quickly to say it, too quickly to capture it, because it's happening while he sees it, and when he discovers it there's already something else to say, there's another light on what he sees, and he has no other alternative than to choose, like any idler, to let things speak for themselves.

Without any enthusiasm for the enthusiasms of others, who talk of the obvious as if it were hidden, reel off commonplaces as if what they were saying had never been written, while the simplicity of a miracle passes right before their eyes. Slightly uneasy about two or three memories he'd like to relate, but can't: partly because they're personal, and partly because they've become flesh of his flesh.

Perhaps these thoughts are not his thoughts, but the ramblings of someone who doesn't admit the reality of his own acts, of his own mind, of his way of understanding his own passage;

perhaps these feelings belong to someone who's in a hurry to get away and sees how, on account of his urgency, distances lengthen, his explanation lengthens, while his imagination runs over and the present erupts and dies in the blink of an eye.

· · ·

Persephone surveys her body with the disconsolate air of a
widow. She sinks into a horizontal well of darkness.
She raises her hands to her head to fix her hair, but
doesn't.
She bites her lips, her fists, and seems to be suffocating.
She closes her eyes, to concentrate or to be alone.
Surrounded by people, she makes a serious effort to become
once more the self she forsook.
She seeks approval that is not forthcoming.
She smiles continuously and for no reason.
She stands up painfully, as if a gradual lucidity were lifting
her.
She looks around her like a woman who feels old and seems
to be taking leave of each object she sees.
She isn't steady on her legs. Her knees give way. She leans
against the wall. She could be walking in her sleep.
She is sweaty yet breathes out cold air.
She wipes off the mascara running into her eyes. The
blended makeup and sweat on her cheeks and neck.
She picks up a doll from a chair. Pulls its straw-colored hair.
Presses it against her bosom.
Her expression when she sees me is one of self-loathing.
She is so forlorn and worn out that she has to stop again for
a few seconds.
She sits down on a chair, still holding the doll. Lights a
cigarette. I breathe in the smell of the match. She blows it
out. Mops the sweat with a napkin.
She drinks the ice from a glass but not the water.
She plays with the doll. Removes its head. Takes out
another doll. Removes its head. Takes out another.
I see her face through the water, through the glass; it grows
thinner, wider, is reduced to a nose, two thick lips.

The cigarette smoke veils her as steam would coming from below, from me, from my mouth, from her curved fingers. I hear the noise that comes before rain, but I don't see the rain.

She fishes a wet paper from the water, the white letters sliding across it, almost invisible. She unfolds it carefully, then tears it without a sound, totally absorbed in the sheer sensation of doing it effortlessly.

She suddenly starts to talk, her emotions spilling out in words. She sticks her finger into a hole in the table, wiggles it; gesticulates with the other hand.

Dresses fall; parties, people fall; love, felt for so long, rises from us, and falls.

She speaks in a voice that is not hers. She speaks as if from another room or another body.

Penumbras become entangled, arms link, the skin shudders, fingernails tear at innocence, love flirts with a shirt, a pair of pants.

She throws the dolls on the floor, they make a hollow, wooden sound, lie prone, supine.

She bends over next to me as if she were pushing aside her own shadow; she seems to rest at last, but only for a moment.

Carnality returns to her features, blood returns to her cheeks. Her breasts jut out disturbingly again, her movements become rhythmical.

She doesn't answer anything I say.

She externalizes a brief annoyance as she leans on her elbows, puts her head in her hands. She looks at the floor as if she were thinking, but she's really laughing.

She breaks the glass. I see the pieces. The sound. What it was. She is struck dumb in the middle of a word.

She clenches her jaws. Mutters between her teeth. Yawns prodigiously.
A waiter leaves some bottles on the other table. I call him, but he doesn't answer me. He doesn't hear me, or he's not interested in me. He doesn't even see me.

Your eyelids close. Are you asleep?
She sighs, tired but amused. Unfit for gentle acts and tender caresses she passes her hand awkwardly over my face.
I can feel the trace of her hair on her fingertips.
I am seeing her as if there were no one but her and God on earth.

The mingled, commingled customers have become a harmonious family of toothy mouths.
They pass each other bottles and glasses, slide their hands over and under necklines, skirts, stockings, thighs.
They only understand what they can touch.
There they are, the miracles of creation, fused into a single, plural blotch, making a multiple, distorted gesture, a uniform pompous noise.
They occupy a time, a thought, a violence.
They lead their lives out of habit, like a mirage that continued looking at makes real.
Their waiting is fearful and clamorous, their reward always seems far off.

The musicians sing and stagger wearily, affably. Their shadows creep along the floor, shrink abruptly, lengthen again.
The dance floor is covered with bare backs and arms, knees, prostitutes and bodies.

Nervous fingers hang on flesh, dig into flesh. A lot of people
are singing. A train whistles.
Magdalena touches me. I don't feel her. She puckers her lips
to kiss my neck. Slavers on me.
They're throwing wine and cigarette butts at Maria's legs.
She backs away, speckled with red and ashes.
Susi is dancing held tight, her eyes shut. Blanca looks on.
Maricarmen looks on.
A fly zooms through the turbid smoke, like an airplane in
the clouds, its flight cradled by the penumbra. Now it alights
on a dirty plate, like a little god of viscosity.
Rosamunda and Marta straddle their chairs, rocking
back and forth as they drink out of a shared bottle. They
sway blithely on the creaking chairs, two crows on a
branch.
The owner counts the whores one by one, like sheep: the
gray one says hello, the blue one makes signs, the red one
frowns, the white one rubs her hip against his shoulder.
Bells and sound peal. The musicians' voices are changing.
An eye squints at me through the window. Presses against
the pane. I am within an idiot's gaze. It goes away.
The handle flows from the body of the pitcher without
interruption or suddenness.
The light bulbs recede toward the darker part of the room,
are specks veiled in smoke.
The blackened mass of night settles over the roof, settles
over the brothel's roots, eases its behind into a chair.
Like a mountain of lethargy, night seeps in, puts on flesh,
walks about passing sentence in the voice of a sniveling
whore. It raises one foot slightly, like a wary deer.
Brushes the hair off its forehead, moves with the
ungainliness of a fat woman.

It tinges walls and windowpanes, pitch-black eyes, belts, is a
teeming dark curtain suspended beyond the windows.

Susi calls out of the thick fog; her voice wriggles across the
room like a creamy snake.
Three times she calls out unheeded, like a widow searching
unconcernedly for a dead man who was never hers.
Time burns outside and inside like a provocation.
The shadows brushing against us smell of dust, have an
ancient feel.
The liquid in that transparent glass is drinking us, the
transparency of that glass is not ours.
The hour when we die will be a dry hour, with poisoned
blood and broken bones.
Termites will nest in lintels, fissures and flesh. Burrowing in
they will split up what looks permanent, what a vision made
us think would last.
Oblivion will cover Maria's bare back, Jazmín's arms and
neck, will unravel veils and stockings, tablecloths and sheets.
The dreamers, the sleepers, the singers and talkers will
succumb, they will lose identity and form, they will be cast
off like strength and caution.
Heads and plates will fall at a gradual speed we cannot
comprehend. Comprehension will succumb in turn, speed,
ignorance will succumb in turn.
The holes in womens' ears will stretch until they become air.
Your love will have no lover, will be only a motionless cavity
in time.
Never again will I see what I am seeing now.
My eyes will be different and the colors I see will be
different.

.   .   .

Susi and Persephone are dancing clasped and entangled,
their hands kindling the coldness at the center of their
bodies.
They move as one, share the same expression.
They advance without getting anywhere, goad each other to
the edge of a line they do not cross; they laugh and sing in
duo.
Their fingers make knots, double fists, their eyes entwine,
their lips brush furtively, they decant their aromas into each
other's mouths. Susi touches her chin to Persephone's neck,
trickles a kiss over her shoulder.
I hear their uneven breathing parting their thighs.
I hear how the nakedness of her breast fondled beneath the
cloth echoes inside Susi.
I dream of what she doesn't dream, I go farther than she
can go, and I return trembling, tired out by the journey she
didn't take, that she didn't think of taking and that she
never, never will take, shielded from the promptings of her
moments, seared by the urgency that forces itself upon her
like something alien.
The hour buries us without echo or reflection, cradles our
memory, our love, shades the place where day soared in its
light and night flew in the stars. Slowly it dissolves, becomes
stranger, weighs in things and bodies as if it were solid.

Noise is heard from the basement. Voices come up. Trickles
of water that rain upwards seep through the ceiling and the
flooring. That water has sound.
There's a party downstairs. An old song plays a scratched
gaiety. The woman singing screeches.
Dishwashers, waiters and busboys are celebrating
underground.

Occasionally a shout comes up, female voices come up,
men's laughter comes up.
The deepest night grinds in the basement.
A demiurge of shadows orchestrates that uproar, sucks down
in a maelstrom the dim radiance that revolves up here.
To go down to it there are only seven steps painted different
colors. We only have to raise the lid of the stepped well and
descend to the bottom.
At the end of this descent the merry sensualists will welcome
us, will whisper in our ear that the real party is downstairs
(not in this din, not in this wink of an eye) although the
darkness from above weighs down constantly.

A shadow line divides Persephone's face.
Sitting down now, she runs her fingers over her legs.
She breathes laboriously, as if catching her breath.
The smoke rises and continues to gush out. There are many
mouths blowing arabesques of smoke and words.
There's a fountain of smoke over the green salad and the
iced drinks.
Many beings emit ashes and noise.
The hours drag me down and the miserable hovels patiently
girdling this landscape, this endless dream of waking men.
The aged children in the dilapidated doorways drag me
down.
I want to get away from memory and the moment, from
Persephone, who sits there like a virtue skulking in its
shadow, from the night that goes out with a thousand hands
and feet hammering in my head.
Outside there are footsteps from neighboring streets, groans
that pierce wooden or cardboard walls on which a name or
an insult has been engraved with knife or pencil.

Above, farther above, there are venetian blinds, curtains
closing in rapid onomatopoeias of sleep.
Down below a dog pulls an old photograph out of the
garbage, a doll, a feather duster.
A drunken beggar holds his hand out into the void, as if he
were receiving coins from a long file of ghosts.

The noisy shadows head for Persephone, turn towards me.
The sleep of fat, greasy animals exhales and snorts the music
of mouths and noses.
Dross and brambles, not cypresses, sprout from the earth
where dawn is nesting. Ivy and bitterness intertwine singing
in this time of wood and stone.
Here fog and lethargy, squandered life and weariness are a
pit.
The moment from which you are fleeing or that you seek is
served to you on a tray by a waiter, a gesture drinks it up
with his wine.
This battered ship only remembers what it hasn't sailed, a
beginning at which you were already old, the distance that
separates you from something you wanted and your own
distance that separates you from yourself.
It only remembers what you would want to remember and no
longer possess.
Now that Persephone assuages the voices of her dream, like
someone who fears hearing her own words.
Because she is no more than an apparition among all the
other apparitions that say yes and no simultaneously to my
irresolute apparition.
She is no more than the person who is there and
smiles, trying to know that she is real and that she is
there.

While the light of cigarettes begins to be invisible in the visible and each body looks like a lonely thought.

The customers emerge from all over, are everywhere; their heads cluster, move apart.
They fumble in the dark like blind drunkards, bump into a back, a breast, a chair.
They fornicate, eat, drink. They gather, scatter. They are a chorus of frogs.
On the brink of copulation they caress reptilian girls, sit them down on their legs and play them as if they were musical instruments.
They are standing or sitting, their eyes come and go, they try to determine who is that man and why he stares at them like that.
The penumbra lights up, the darkness goes out. Loud and shrill voices divide up the air.
They will disperse at dawn when the bells are rung.

The sun dissolves clots of darkness on other ground. Other eyes discover in daylight what was hidden.
Somewhere a cloud is already white. The sun already decks out trees in nimble proportions.
Elsewhere the miracle is sheer earth.
Love raises up bodies from every surface.

Through the window, day falls on my left cheek: tears of light run down it.
Everything around me is sailing, everything is unsteady under my feet.
The floorboards creak like a box on stilts.
I have rained and I have watched for thirty-six hours.

I have prayed beneath this reflected, subordinate light.
I have seen that my desire is a stranger under the sun.
The movement, the shapes that morning discloses are only
embodied rubbish, stones with eyes.
What the light finds are only astounded dead men.

There where the white gauzes of fog watch,
this was what I said.
And what I saw, I didn't see, but another: the one who is
there, where the net of air traps the bird, and nobody sees
us or knows us.

ABOUT THE AUTHOR AND THE TRANSLATOR

HOMERO ARIDJIS was born in Contepec, Michocan, Mexico, in 1940, to a Greek father and Mexican mother. Generally recognized as Mexico's most distinguished poet among his generation, Aridjis is the author of numerous volumes of verse and three novels. He has been awarded a Guggenheim prize and has lived in Spain and Paris. He now resides in Mexico with his American wife.

BETTY FERBER was born in New York City, spent several years in Europe, and now lives in Mexico City. She has edited a critical anthology of Marcel Proust and translated a number of Homero Aridjis's poems for the collection *Blue Spaces*. She coordinated the translations for the Festival Internacional de Poesía (Morelia, 1981) and the Encuentro Internacional de Poesía (Mexico City, 1982).